South San Francisco Public Library
W9-BZW-508

dead upon a time

dead upon a time

ELIZABETH PAULSON

SCHOLASTIC PRESS / NEW YORK

Library of Congress Cataloging-in-Publication Data available

ISBN 978-0-545-64046-6

10 9 8 7 6 5 4 3 2 1   15 16 17 18 19

Printed in the U.S.A.   23
First edition, September 2015

Book design by Nina Goffi

For Cormac and Maeve,
who slept so soundly
while I wrote these pages.

CHAPTER 1

Not for the first time while trekking up the steepest part of Birch Hill, Kate Hood wished her boots had been sewn onto slightly thicker soles. She stuck to the center of Woodson Road, the part most traveled by carriage and coach, but still felt every pebble and puddle beneath her feet. She knew that, by the time she kicked loose the boots and peeled off her woolen socks in front of the crackling hearth at Nan's house, her toes would be blue and numb.

As if it sensed her longing for warmth, the wind chose that moment to pick up. Kate swore softly and drew her cloak tight around her shoulders. *Pointless to turn back now*, she chided herself. Shepherd's Grove and its collection of thatched roofs and puffing chimneys sat two miles down the hill she'd just climbed. How many times had she and Nan argued over the remote location of Nan's cozy stone cottage?

"It's dangerous," Kate had insisted to her grandmother. "There's no reason to live so far from the rest of the village."

"What would you have me do, Katie?" Nan had answered. "Cart my house down the hill, piece by piece, and rebuild it in the village square?"

"There are other houses." Kate had pressed the matter. "Why even keep a whole cottage? The village is full of establishments with perfectly lovely rooms to rent."

Nan had scoffed at that idea. "You'd have me living in the cellar of the town tavern!"

The image of Kate's grandmother bedding down among the kegs and wine casks in the tavern's basement had stirred them both to giggles. And once again, the matter of Nan's isolation had been swept aside, along with several other topics that made them both uneasy.

Kate knew that Nan's brothers had built the cottage for her decades ago, when her grandmother was younger. Back then, living on her own in the middle of the shaded glen must have seemed exhilarating, even romantic. Nan had her reasons, Kate reminded herself, for seeking a life on the outskirts. She'd heard bits and pieces over the years and understood that the more predictable citizens of Shepherd's Grove had been only too happy to see Nan put down roots a good distance away.

The distance is made of more than just miles, Kate thought now. The farther she traveled up the mountain, the denser the woods grew. Shadows replaced sunlight. She heard owls instead of songbirds and saw bare tree branches stretched out like bony hands from the shallow mounds of dead leaves. *Beauty in gloom is still beauty*—Nan was fond of that saying. Each time a branch crackled under Kate's feet and startled her, she repeated the familiar phrase and tried to calm herself. After all, it wouldn't do for someone with her bloodline to be spooked by a common forest.

She didn't have a wise proverb to counteract the cold wind, though. Kate gritted her teeth against the bitter freeze. Nan could chuckle all she liked about moving house, but she wasn't the one trudging up and down Birch Hill, lugging a full basket of groceries. She had Kate to serve as her errand girl. Not to mention the fact that it might be pleasant—it might actually be comforting—to have some family living in town instead of just drifting around as Kate Hood, resident tragic orphan.

When Kate first heard the low growl beneath the gusts of wind, she half believed it was the grumble of her own resentment. But then she heard another snarl. And another. Her skin prickled with sudden vigilance and she sucked in her breath, willing her heartbeat to slow to silence. It was the slight yip tacked on to the next growl that iced her veins. She would know that particular call anywhere. Wolves. And from the sound of it, the whole pack had encircled her.

Kate cursed the bundles of meat and cheese packed into her basket. Even if the beasts didn't pick up the scent of her fear, they would still latch on to the aroma of smoked venison and aged cheddar. *You have no choice,* she commanded herself. Fighting was her only option.

After hauling the heavy load up the mountain, it pained her to toss the food to the snarling circle of wolves. All that effort would be devoured in seconds. Better the groceries than her, though. The carefully wrapped packages bought Kate some time. As the wolves tore into the venison and cheese, she drew her knife out of the sheath carefully woven into the side of her basket. When the first wolf lunged at her, she was ready for him.

The dark gloom suddenly worked to Kate's advantage. It allowed her to focus, first on the glittering yellow eyes of the pack leader and then on the blade she brandished in front of her. In the dim shadows of the deep woods, Kate's knife whistled through the air in an arc of metal. She connected right below the animal's breastbone, and the wolf collapsed in a heap of matted fur.

As Kate wrenched her knife out of the first wolf's dense muscle, two more attacked. She swiped at one and kicked at the other, barely registering as its fangs sank into the skin of her ankle. When she did feel the bite, she yelped and kicked harder. Her cries didn't sound so different from those of the wounded beasts dropping away from her. Still, Kate knew that if she failed to dominate, the whole pack would set upon her. So she did what she had to. She became the predator.

Her blade found its targets. Her two assailants slunk away with their silver tails dragging along the ground. Their cohorts licked their chops, seemed to gauge Kate, her knife, and the wounds of the injured before they, too, decided to back off. Once they were gone, Kate leaned against a white birch and tried to catch her breath. She no longer felt the cold. Instead, she could not stop her hands from shaking.

What a mess. Kate took stock of the torn paper scattered around the forest floor—the only remnants of the provisions that had weighed down her heavy basket. Nan would shrug it off, she knew. But it meant another freezing slog up Birch Hill in the near future. The bite on Kate's ankle throbbed in protest.

She almost let herself collapse right there in the clearing—but the growls and yips off in the distance reminded her she couldn't simply sit and wait for the pack to return. Every step hurt, but the sounds of the wolves spurred Kate to scurry faster. She thought again of Nan's warm hearth. Kate knew her grandmother would first fold her into her outstretched arms and then fuss over the wound on her ankle.

When Kate finally saw the two myrtle trees that flanked the cottage's front walk, her legs gave out a little. She suddenly felt how tired she was, how scared she'd been.

She enjoyed a few seconds of security before getting close enough to realize that something was terribly wrong. The heavy oak door of the cottage hung open, as if gaping in surprise.

"Nan?" she called out hesitantly. Had her grandmother heard the wolves' howls and come outside to investigate? Kate crossed the front walk and stepped across the threshold into a chill even colder than the windy woods outside. The oil lamps flickered and the fire had died down to cinders. She saw a pot poised over the hearth; peeking inside, she found its contents blackened, the broth boiled off. A wooden spoon had fallen and lay near the shards of a white ceramic bowl. Kate pictured her grandmother's bony and spotted hands releasing the bowl, wielding the spoon in measly defense.

It wasn't wolves. Kate reminded herself that the creatures she'd tangled with minutes before wouldn't have left food simmering. They would have shredded the woolen blankets in Nan's favorite chair and tracked mud all through the pristine home.

Once more, Kate shivered. This time the chill started deep in her spine and radiated out, causing her whole body to buckle and straighten.

The cold that surrounded her now wasn't weather. It was evil.

Kate knew it well.

CHAPTER 2

"Nan? Nan!" Kate couldn't resist darting through the small rooms of the house, calling for her grandmother. Aside from the yawning front door, the cottage was sealed shut. Nan had even lined the windowsills with flannel sheets to cut down on the drafts whistling through.

Other than the spoon and the broken bowl, Kate didn't find any sign of a struggle. That worried her most of all. Nan was a fighter—if she'd been overtaken in her own home, she would have left a trail of blood. Hers or her intruder's. "NAN!" Kate bellowed with all the strength left in her voice. In case someone or something was dragging her grandmother away right then, she wanted Nan to know she was already searching.

Kate kept screaming as she scanned each room. She looked for anything out of place, anything different. She stopped short when she caught a glimpse of the northeast corner of Nan's bedroom.

This was where her grandmother liked to weave. She had set up a stool right in front of several looms. Kate knew she'd been learning different techniques in recent weeks, and the work on the four looms right now could only be called stunning. The more Kate stared, the more she found the tapestries mesmerizing. The scenes they illustrated definitely counted as creepy. Kate felt the temperature drop even further as she studied them.

Each half-finished loom depicted a prison cell. Kate could tell by the gray brick walls and the barred windows positioned well above any inmate's height. Nan had chosen to stream threads of sunlight through each window. It added a sense of hope to the dark scenes.

And each scene was darker than the one before. In the first, a raven-haired beauty sat at a wooden table. Along the table's scarred top stood a dozen apples. The girl looked terrified as she reached for the apple in the center of the table. She seemed to examine the fruit as if it could kill her.

The tapestry to the left of that featured a boy or a girl—Kate couldn't tell for sure. The prisoner had the delicate features and ornate dress of a young aristocratic woman, but also the shaven head of a captive soldier. She/he sat forlornly on the floor, gazing through the bars of the window, holding a comb in one hand.

Next was a scene with a boy and a girl locked away with only each other for comfort. They looked flushed with heat—Kate could see where her grandmother had embroidered red and orange flames licking the walls and floor of their cell. The pair clutched at each other as their faces contorted with pain.

The last tapestry looked as if it had demanded the most intricate handiwork. Kate saw it and gasped. With her auburn hair curling around her face, and enormous green eyes welling with tears, the girl kneeling in the center of the dim room was truly beautiful. But the setting was even more so. It looked as if every surface of the cell had been covered with needles or nails—sharp metal glinting sinisterly. Nan must have used silver thread, for it glittered against the scene's dark backdrop. *Beauty in gloom is still beauty.* Kate could almost hear her grandmother whispering as she stitched.

There was no arguing with her grandmother's artistry, but Kate couldn't stand to face the tapestries any longer. Whatever they were, whatever ember of imagination had inspired them, they frightened her. They looked too well sewn—as if Nan had pried open a window into the suffering of actual prisoners, and the prisoners had found a way to weave their own stories through her aging, arthritic hands.

So Kate turned away and retraced her steps through the cottage. Past the broken bowl and the stranded spoon. Past the abandoned pot and the dying fire. And that's when she saw it: hanging in a needlework hoop, tacked onto the inside of Nan's front door. It was just a scrap of fabric—plain white muslin. The kind of material her grandmother would have used to fashion herself a nightgown.

The lettering curved and drooped, a distorted version of her grandmother's sure hand. Someone unpracticed had sewn it. The letters looked like scratches, breaking the taut skin of the cotton. Her name wasn't threaded anywhere, but Kate knew with absolute certainty the message was meant for her.

Kate plucked the needlepoint off the door and traced it with one trembling finger.

It was supposed to be you.

CHAPTER 3

Kate's vision blurred and her legs felt like liquid. She sensed the tendrils of hysteria emerging within her. *Nan needs me,* she reminded herself, and that steadied her, the steely reality at her core. She glanced around the humble cottage. The framed pictures on the mantel housed the faces of family long gone. Nan's lack of neighbors left Kate with little choice—she needed to find help in the village.

This time, Kate didn't bother keeping to the path. She blazed through the woods, fighting through bramble patches and dense weeds. Some of the thorny branches scratched her face. Some of the weeds felt like razors against her shins.

Kate's lungs burned and her side ached from sprinting. Her leg still ached from the wolf bite, although it felt like days since the creatures' teeth had sunk into her skin. She couldn't help but chide herself as she fought through the wilderness. To think that less than an hour before, she'd been worried about lost groceries. What was wrong with her?

When her mind raced forward faster than her feet, she almost stopped short right in the middle of a thornbush. What would she do once she reached town? Who would she ask for help?

Close enough to see the roofs of the village houses, Kate thought, *It looks so welcoming from up here.* Clusters of buildings stood like bunches of partygoers chatting. She saw the peaked roof of the chapel in the center of the village, and the glassy blue water of the town reservoir. Sometimes, she saw girls gathered at the side of the water, washing their families' laundry. They seemed so comfortable together, laughing behind their hands. Maybe for them, Shepherd's Grove was a friendly place. They bought on credit in the town's shops and ate supper at one another's tables. They glided through town, feeling perfectly at ease, perfectly at home.

For her, Shepherd's Grove was different. It wasn't a friendly place. In her heart, Kate knew that. Just as she would never dare to join a circle of village girls at the side of the water or sit beside them at church, Kate didn't expect finding help would be easy. Something terrible had torn through the cottage uphill, though, taking her grandmother with it. For Nan's sake, she had to try. Kate gritted her teeth, bowed her head, and forced her way through the last of the thickets surrounding the low hills of Shepherd's Grove.

She had planned to quietly and swiftly track down the town elders. But when she burst into the pretty shaded lanes, she found herself screaming, "Help me, please! Someone, please! Help me!" The words burst from her lips like alarms. But who would hear? Stumbling up the walk, Kate was surprised to see the streets so empty. Dusk usually counted as a busy time in town, as residents moved from their homes to the pub or visited with one another on the wooden benches perched outside so many of their homes.

Where was everyone? Kate sifted through her memory—was it some kind of feast day? She shook her head. She remembered bounding out of bed that morning. The only special element of the day was the trip to see Nan. She called out loudly, but more calmly, "Please? Would someone help me? Hello?" She tried, "I don't mean to disturb the supper hour." But the town remained still and silent. She didn't even hear the clanging of pots, the scrape of forks against plates.

Kate ran her shaky fingers through her hair and pulled out several burs, some loose leaves, even a few tiny branches. *I must look a fright,* she thought. Breathing deeply, she realized her face stung from more than holding back tears. She felt along her cheeks and found scratches along her skin. She had run so fast, she hadn't even realized how the thick brush had torn up her face. A quick check of her clothes revealed rips and tears there, too. Blood had seeped through the cloth she'd tied around her bitten ankle.

Kate quickly tried to straighten herself out. Maybe her neighbors didn't recognize her as the quiet girl who'd worked odd jobs and lived in a string of spare rooms for most of her life. Maybe they'd seen her tearing through the forest and considered her some kind of beast.

Kate made herself slow down and think rationally. No one had a chance to be put off by her appearance. Shepherd's Grove had been sealed as tightly as a tomb when she arrived. And despite the quiet and the resolutely shuttered windows, plumes of smoke blew from each residence's chimney. The villagers were all home, safe and secure in front of their carefully tended fireplaces.

They were afraid. They already knew Kate needed help and had chosen to shut themselves away instead. Well, she wouldn't make it easy for them. Kate began banging on doors, moving quickly from cottage to cottage. She pounded each wooden door with both hands, calling out, "Please, help! Won't someone please help?" At the seamstress's home, where she'd once rented a room and worked as a lackey, she called out, "Agnes, please! It's Kate Hood! Please help me!" Nothing.

At Dr. Owen's home, she yelled, "Emergency! Please! I'm injured!" But no one opened the door and ushered her in for treatment or comfort.

Outside Reverend Jacob's expansive cabin, Kate sank to her knees at the front steps. "Help me, please! Someone, help!" She paused for a second and then dared to tack on, "For the love of God, please help me!" But even invoking the name of God didn't pry open the heavy mahogany door of the Reverend's home.

Kate sank back and leaned against the closed door. She ducked her head and allowed herself a few soft sobs. Above her, black clouds had rolled in, cloaking Shepherd's Grove in shadow. Regaining herself, Kate stood up, brushed the dust off her knees, and started attacking doors again. She slammed her fists against the wooden shutters. "Help me, please! Someone, come help!" She didn't care if she looked crazy—the villagers could think what they wanted of her, as long as someone stepped forward to help. "Please, help me! Have mercy and help!"

"You're going to need mercy if you wake up my baby girl." Kate heard the growled threat and stopped in her tracks. To her left, on the porch of a shabby cabin a few doors down, a tiny woman wearing a calico kerchief over her hair sat on an overturned pail. Kate recognized the woman who raised goats and sold their milk at the weekly market. Dinah Flanders treated most of the villagers like dirt she'd tracked indoors from her barn. For as long as Kate could remember, Dinah had gazed at her as if she were a particularly offensive smudge. She didn't think the diminutive goatherd had ever before actually addressed her personally. Kate wasn't even sure she'd heard her correctly.

"I'm sorry?"

"You will be. Mark my words if you wake up that baby."

"I didn't know you had a baby."

"Oh, yeah? You didn't get the christening invitation?" Dinah snorted meanly, and Kate felt her face flush with embarrassment.

Out of the entire village, the only person sitting outside happened to be the most ferocious. Kate thought she'd rather sit and chat with the pack of wolves. She closed her eyes wearily. "Please." She could not keep the whimper out of her voice. "I need help. Something terrible has happened to my grandmother."

Dinah held up her hand. "Stop. Please."

But it was the one crack Kate had found in the sealed vault of Shepherd's Grove. She had to try to claw through. "My Nan is all I have. When I was a little baby like your girl, Nan was the one who rocked me to sleep, who sang me songs."

"I can only imagine the songs that creature sang to you."

"You must have never met my Nan. She keeps a cottage right over that hill. She's very brave, living on her own at her age. You probably hadn't been born the last time my grandmother came down the mountain. So you might not know—"

"We all know who she is." Dinah's voice was clipped and cold. "And we know what she is. Eventually, evil tends to take care of evil. I don't know if you're a fool or a fraud, but it's plain enough that you're not welcome here in Shepherd's Grove." Dinah stood up, turned the bucket she'd been sitting on right side up, and loudly spit in it. "If you had any sense, you'd stop banging on doors and raising a ruckus. Slink back off into the woods, like your grandma once did."

Kate refused to let the goatherd see how these scathing words scarred her spirit. She kept her eyes on the thick curl of smoke drifting from the chimney of Reverend Jacob's home. She wouldn't cry. She wouldn't let herself become a story Dinah Flanders bragged about at the village well. She heard Dinah's door creak closed and the scrape of the dead bolt sliding into place. Only then did Kate let a few tears escape.

Just as she did, the darkened sky opened up, pouring rain. A furious wind whipped in a frenzy. Kate didn't bother attempting to shield herself. What was the use? Sometimes weather was just weather—she knew that. But her grandmother had taught her that a good storm could also mean tumult in the spirit world. She imagined Nan wailing for help and those cries spinning themselves into a tornado.

Somehow, I will find you, Kate silently swore to Nan. She forced herself to stand up straight and walk back to the forest's edge. Even as she stepped into the brush, she maintained her proud posture. She would not allow Dinah the satisfaction of watching her skulk away into the deep recesses of the forest.

Once Kate reached the cover of trees, she ducked. Her tattered clothing clung to her rain-soaked body. She stood shivering, hoping the dense pines would provide some kind of canopy to protect her from the downpour. In her heart, Kate knew that climbing back up that mountain would spell Nan's death and her own eventual isolation. She could go back to her grandmother's cottage and comfort herself living among Nan's things. But she knew that meant signing on for years of loneliness. She wouldn't kid herself, as Nan might have done so many years ago. The trip wouldn't be temporary.

Besides, those tapestries were back there. Even the thought of them rolled up and shoved into the far corner of a closet creeped her out. Kate couldn't unsee them. Each time she shut her eyes against the storm, she saw the vivid and violent scenes her grandmother had woven. They haunted her. And the thought that somewhere, Nan herself was living through a similar torture tormented Kate. She couldn't quit searching. She couldn't give up on her grandmother.

She might have to give up on Shepherd's Grove, though. That left her with few options. But Kate could think of only one person who might understand—the only person, in fact, who might count as an even bigger outcast.

Now she had to find him.

CHAPTER 4

Kate had only a vague inkling of Jack's location, by his own design. As quickly as word got out that his warren of rooms existed in the shade of a wisteria bush or beside a patch of thyme, the vegetation changed. Jack switched it easily and often.

Had he avoided certain circumstances, many of the local farmers would have considered Jack a sought-after apprentice. He showed such promise that he might even have been given a parcel of land by his eighteenth birthday. But Jack's mother had taken ill and he hadn't thought he could wait until he turned eighteen to try to change the direction of the heavy pendulum of their fortunes. And that decision had earned him the scorn of the entire village.

Kate didn't know what to expect—how Jack might react if she sought out his bunker. But she could at least count on him to understand why she must risk everything for Nan's safety.

She knew it was useless to call for him. If anything, Jack might tunnel out and disappear farther into the forest recesses. Instead, Kate looked for signs, as if she were tracking deer—bent branches, strawberry plants stripped of fruit. She searched for hours, sometimes on her knees. A few times, she crawled under a snarl of vines, only to find nothing but dirt on the other side. As she tracked and crawled and dug around here and there, the cold rain kept falling. Kate could feel her very bones clatter when she moved, as if they were so frozen, they might shatter with a jolt to one of her joints. Her fingertips had become like prunes, as if she'd sat in the bath too long. But no, she thought ruefully, a bath would be warm. A bath would be lovely.

Kate remembered how she had been streaked with dirt during her recent stand in Shepherd's Grove. She had felt so self-conscious, certain she would frighten the locals. Now, three hours into her search for Jack, she was covered in dirt, with an occasional streak of clean. The dirt wedged under her fingernails seemed permanently implanted. She tasted mud and felt just about ready to let herself sink into it, when she noticed a blanket of moss that didn't lie quite so flat on a bed of smooth shale. She dragged her body over to it.

It was more than just a blanket of moss—it was a quilt created with a skill that rivaled her grandmother's. Kate could see that the pieces were sewn together with long blades of grass. Someone had taken care to keep the stitches tiny and precise. She handled the work gently, slowly drawing it to the side and folding it over on itself. The mossy curtain revealed a long sheet of shale, which she nudged over to the side.

Found you.

Kate leaned forward, peering down into the steep drop below. She could vaguely make out the shadows of a stool and a table.

"Jack?" she called out in a slight whisper that quickly turned to a gasp as she felt a sharp blade dig between her shoulders.

Before she could react, she felt herself being shoved forward, to lean precariously over the deep pit.

"Best not to move a muscle," a voice hissed. "One twist of my knife and you'll have no choice but to crawl around in the dirt for the rest of your days." And then almost as an afterthought, the voice added, "You little worm."

It was the insult rather than the threat that convinced Kate it was Jack Haricot himself pinning her down and dangling her over the steep hollow of his hideaway. She recognized the needling voice from their childhood disputes. Back then, he hounded and plagued her. But those were the good old days, when the worst that could happen was she'd have to eat her lunch by herself.

When she spoke up, she pretended to be back in the village, taunting him while they were both supposed to be earning their keep on some farmer's burgeoning acreage.

"Hey, Jack, that's a heck of a way to get a girl into your room." Kate said it lightly, but she still braced herself, waiting to fall.

"I've got better things to do, I assure you. Let me guess. The other little girls dared you to come out here. And do what? Steal a lock of my hair? Create a map leading the whole village back to the only place where I feel safe? What an adventurer you are!" Jack spat out the next words over Kate's protests. "How brave!"

Kate wriggled and stretched in order to turn her body to face him. He let her squirm, but repositioned the knife at the base of her throat. She swallowed against it. *Not exactly an improvement.* "You really don't remember me, do you?" Kate searched his eyes, silently willing him to see past the mess of mud and tears. She tried again. "I'm not really the kind of girl the others invite into their circle."

Jack looked down at her warily. "You don't seem to mind showing up here without an invitation." Then he peered more closely at her and startled in recognition. "Katie?"

Kate sighed. "It's Kate now, actually."

"Ah, the second syllable went by way of the pigtails. Very sophisticated." Jack said it wryly, but Kate could feel him regarding her, measuring how she'd grown. She felt grateful to be coated in mud. She'd rather tumble down into the darkness than simply sit there blushing like some moron while Jack Haricot held a knife at her neck.

She glared down at it as if her current predicament were the blade's fault. "Exactly. So maybe we can both be civilized?"

Jack went quiet. His eyes shifted to either side. Kate felt, for one brief gasp of a moment, the knife's blade press back into her skin. He asked, "How do I know they didn't send you?"

"Who? The villagers?" Kate laughed at the suggestion, but mirthlessly, for the wounds Dinah Flanders had inflicted still smarted. "They'd never ask for my help. Not with anything. They hate me."

"Probably not as much as they hate me," Jack said—but at the same time, he relented, sitting back and easing off her slightly. Kate heard the metallic click of the switchblade folding back into its case. "It's not safe for you to be here." Jack leaned against the tree and gazed morosely off into the distance. "And I need to ask: Any chance you could have been followed?"

Kate thought back to the rows of sealed doors in Shepherd's Grove and the accompanying eerie silence. "No way. No one followed me. They practically drove me out with clubs and torches." She grimaced and immediately wished she could reel the words back into her mouth. The last thing she needed was for Jack to think she was mocking him. Or that she endorsed the callous way he'd once been treated. Kate tried to repair the damage. "I mean, they made it clear that I wasn't welcome there."

Jack continued to look away. "Yeah? What did you do to incur the wrath of the Great Community?" He chewed his lip and glared at the scattered collection of chimneys in the distance.

"I was born, I guess." Kate shrugged. "Into a family they don't approve of. Then I had the audacity to ask for help." Jack shook his hair, scattering droplets of water. The rain had tapered to a mist, and Kate felt grateful for that. At least she hadn't exposed his home to the pounding rain when she found the secret entrance. She looked balefully at him. It didn't feel right to ask this lonely boy for anything, but Kate had nowhere else to turn.

Just as her lips were about to form the word *please*, Jack sprang to his feet, into a crouching position. "Well, I suppose you'll tell me about it eventually." He braced a hand on either side of the hollow and deftly dropped down. "You need to remember to duck your head down here," Jack called up to Kate. "High ceilings didn't make it onto my list of priorities."

Kate wasn't about to spend a lot of time debating whether or not she should disappear into a dark, underground bunker with the local town pariah. She sat with her legs hanging into the lip of the hole, shut her eyes, then plunged down. She hit the floor faster than she expected and heard the wicked crack of her ankle snap under her weight. "Ooohhh," she groaned, clutching at it with her frozen hands.

"What did I just tell you?" Jack scolded, shaking his head with dismay.

I will not cry, Kate swore to herself. *I will* not *cry.* She hopped up as best she could, careful not to put too much weight on her right side.

"You mentioned high ceilings," she replied. "Not shallow floors." As her eyes adjusted to the dim light, she was able to discern shapes from shadows. Jack had built quite a home for himself. Some of it—the discarded clothing and scattered checker pieces in one corner—looked exactly how she'd expect the boy who'd once tied her shoelaces together to organize himself. But some things, like the carved stools and the table crafted from a Shepherd's Grove town sign, she couldn't help but admire.

Oil lamps threw silhouetted designs on the walls. The lamps, refashioned jam jars, hung from bent horseshoes. Kate noticed several stuffed feed sacks piled into a hollow in the deepest recesses of the cavern. "You're not living off of animal feed, are you, Jack?" she asked.

He followed her gaze. "Nah. That's my bedroom." He strode over, picked up a feed sack, and hurled it at her. Kate's arms instinctively swung up, ready to knock down a forty-pound bag of cracked corn. Instead, she found herself clutching a soft pillow. She watched Jack grab a second feed sack and unbutton the side. He gathered up the clothes from the floor and shoved them inside. "You see, it's a perfect system. I can pick up my clothes and make up my bed at the same time."

Kate sniffed, determined to avoid showing how impressed she was. "I hope you're sorting the clean from the dirty."

"I live underground. Like a mole. I smell earthy at best."

"I figured you'd build a tree house."

"And that's why I'm so brilliant. So did everyone else. Most of the mobs who first came through barely looked down." He straddled a tree-trunk stool. "Besides, I'm not one for heights any longer."

"I'm sorry."

"For what?"

Kate didn't know where to begin. For the loss of his mom, because she knew how lonely and lost being motherless felt. For the terrible way the town had turned on him—blaming him for the rage unleashed by a colossal assailant whom they could not control. For her own indifference. The truth was that for most of the past year and a half, Jack Haricot had never even crossed her mind. She didn't wonder how he battled hunger most evenings when she sat down to her own supper. Last winter, she hadn't worried whether Jack was safe and warm.

Finally, she told him. "I'm sorry that no one stood up for you." Kate corrected herself. "That I didn't stand up for you."

Jack ducked his head. "Ah, Kate Hood, something tells me you've had enough to worry over. Don't spend that concern on me." He gently pushed a second stool closer to her. "Have a seat before you bonk your head on my tin-can chandelier."

Kate looked up to see an elaborate contraption, built from several cans, clipped and bent to look like the petals of blossoming flowers.

"I only light it on special occasions, since it uses up so many candles."

Kate blushed again, to her mortification. *You're here to get help for Nan,* she chided herself. *Not to make eyes at an outcast boy who simply feels sorry for you.*

She concentrated on the fact that it felt good to sit down. The ankle she had twisted on the way down into Jack's rabbit hole was the same one that had been gnawed on by the boldest of the wolf pack earlier in the day. And it wasn't just her ankle. Kate ached with weariness. She'd been operating on desperation for most of the day. She blurted out, "Jack, you have to help me." Because otherwise she feared she'd collapse in a heap on the dirt floor.

"I guess that's another reason I'm sorry," Kate continued. "Because I'm only here now that I need something. Not from any generous place in my heart."

Jack looked away then. He gazed up toward the ceiling at the busy and distant world above. Kate sighed. How foolish to risk being honest when the stakes were so high.

"Well, you're lucky I'm so desperate for a friend, then." Jack leveled his gaze at her, and Kate felt her ungenerous heart lurch just a little bit in her chest. *Stop it*, she told herself again as Jack went on. "And before you go beating yourself up over it, most folks from Shepherd's Grove wouldn't trust me enough to ask for my assistance. So that's something I appreciate."

Inexplicably, Kate felt her eyes tear up. Jack might not know what he was signing up for. And it was entirely possible that even with his help, Nan was lost to her forever. But she no longer felt so alone in facing whatever nameless, faceless force had stolen the one source of comfort from her life. She had an actual, genuine, giant killer standing beside her now.

Kate scooted her stool closer to Jack's.

"All right," she said, "here's all I know."

CHAPTER 5

When she wrapped up her story, Jack raised his eyebrows.

"That's it? That's not a whole lot to go on, Kate. Are you sure she didn't just change plans at the last second? You're worried, yes, but your Nan has only been missing a good six hours."

"It hasn't been a good six hours, actually." Kate tried to keep her voice light. "Nan doesn't leave that mountain. The farthest she travels is a few yards into her garden." She could see him weighing these facts against his own doubt. "Nan's like us in a way. They might have driven you underground, but they sent her up that mountain. All alone. Surrounded by wolves and lord knows what else."

"The wolf pack is an interesting piece." Jack steepled his fingers in front of his pursed lips, thinking.

"My ankle found them fascinating."

"When was the last time you were attacked by wolves?"

"This morn—"

"Before that?" He sighed in exasperation.

Kate shook her head. "Well, never. But I was carrying Nan's grocery order. They must have smelled the food and circled."

"But that couldn't have been the first time you did a food run for your grandma, right? Wolves don't normally hunt people. We're far too much bother for them. All these months, I've been burrowed into the deepest parts of the forest and I've never faced wolf trouble."

"Yeah, but—"

"*Except* for the times that hunting parties have passed through. Then, suddenly, I hear howls. It sounds to me like something put your wolves on high alert. Something really frightening. It left them confused and defensive, and then you came strolling along. Maybe the smell of food was just a welcome distraction."

Kate considered it. She grudgingly admitted the theory had a certain logic. "I can't go back and ask the wolves, though."

"No, of course not. Wolves hate to be interviewed. But that's information we can keep in mind. Whatever we're trying to track scared the dickens out of a pack of wolves. Doesn't that make you feel better?"

"Not for Nan."

Jack switched back to solemn mode. "No, not for your Nan. Or the others, for that matter."

"What others?"

He looked baffled for a moment. Then conflicted. Finally, he took a deep breath. "Your grandmother's not the only one who has gone missing. It started a while back, before—well, before the giant."

"What started?"

"The disappearances." Jack studied her. "That's been a bit of a topic in Shepherd's Grove, you know. The sudden surge of the missing. You haven't heard anything about that?" Kate shook her head. "Well, for a while, my own . . . drama might have overshadowed it." Jack sighed again and looked down at his lap.

Kate almost pointed out that the villagers in Shepherd's Grove barely spoke to her, let alone filled her in on the town gossip. But she didn't want to say anything that might slow down Jack's revelations. Instead, she leaned forward so far on her stool that she almost toppled off it.

He took a deep breath and began again. "For a while now, people have been vanishing. All kinds of people. Not just old ladies living on the outskirts of town. It started with a girl a few years older than me. I remember because, honestly, I was a bit sweet on her. She had the longest hair I'd ever seen. Anyway, her parents made an initial fuss. They organized search parties; I volunteered to be part of one, even though I was all of twelve back then. Then, just as suddenly, her whole family stopped talking about her. They took down all the drawings of her face and stopped asking folks traveling through if they'd glimpsed her on their journeys.

"My mother told me that perhaps she'd gotten herself in trouble or run off with a boy from a nearby township. That made sense enough, although it chipped away at me. She was so lovely. I could only imagine she'd been lured away by someone older and stronger than me.

"But then, another girl, a neighbor of hers, disappeared a few months later. It's been mostly young girls who've vanished, right at the cusp of womanhood." Jack coughed self-consciously. "Like you, I suppose. Apparently, that's a dangerous time for girls. I had thought only animals were hunted. That's a frightening thing to grow up feeling, I imagine." He looked at her for confirmation, but Kate only shrugged. She'd never felt like other young girls, after all. For the briefest of moments, she allowed herself to remember the note she'd found, but then forced herself to listen more closely to Jack. It wouldn't do to allow herself to be carried away by girlish frights.

Jack continued, "The curious piece, though, was the silence. After Zelda, no one organized any search parties. People barely spoke about the girls who later went missing. Not until it began affecting even younger children—"

"A boy and girl, right? Brother and sister?"

Jack's eyebrows shot up. "That's right. So you *do* know about some of these cases."

Yes and no. Kate debated telling Jack about the tapestries. He'd offered her help. He'd welcomed her into his home. She couldn't expect him to trust her and then keep such an enormous secret from him. But she also knew what the detail on those tapestries implied. A stranger might easily draw the conclusion that her grandmother was re-creating a view she had seen with her own eyes. Or that the images represented Nan's own twisted fantasies. Was Jack still a stranger, though? Would he really jump to those grim assumptions?

Kate closed her eyes and took a leap. "There's something else you should know." She did her best to describe the scenes on the tapestries—the vivid expressions of pain and terror on the children's faces, the detailed torture.

When she finished, Jack let loose a low whistle. "And you know your grandmother created them?"

She tilted her head, remembering the art stretched out on easels and hanging from walls. "They're hers."

"No chance that someone else could have sent them to her? As a threat?"

Which would be worse? It didn't really matter, since Kate knew the truth. "I know she created them. I just don't understand what could have inspired them."

"What do you know about your grandmother?"

"I know she's not evil. She doesn't build torture chambers for children and then weave commemorative wall hangings about them."

"But you do know she's Uncommon?"

Kate's breath caught. No one had ever directly spoken that word to her before. She'd often heard it murmured in her presence. And once, when she heard the village girls taunting each other with it, she had asked Nan what it meant.

"Well, *uncommon* means extraordinary," her grandmother had answered lightly, never betraying the magnitude of the term or the effect that the one word had had on her own life. "It's used to highlight something special."

But the girls hadn't been shouting compliments at each other. Kate knew this, and pieced together what she could. She knew that *common* traditionally referred to those without any royal blood coursing through their veins. She figured *Uncommon* ranked somewhere between royal and common.

As she'd grown older, she understood the discomfort others had with the term. Most adults couldn't seem to pronounce it without hushing their voices. And the more they whispered, the more carefully Kate listened. When Amos Bammell's dairy cows all took ill and died, she knew the villagers attributed it to the Uncommon in their midst. Same thing when a tornado took off the chapel's original steeple. Or that terrible February people kept visiting the town well only to draw up a bucket filled with blood instead of water.

"People believe my grandmother is Uncommon." Kate kept her tone matter-of-fact. "That's why she lived almost five hard-hiking miles across the mountain. That's why I went to the market for her." *Because the grocer refused to take her money,* Kate didn't add. "It's also why I was so alone so much of the time. Nan didn't want the whole village to associate me with her. She let me distance myself from her in hopes they might give me a chance."

"But they didn't give you much of a chance." Jack spoke quietly.

"No, they didn't. I don't know why Nan ever expected them to." They certainly hadn't given Kate's mother that opportunity years before. But Kate didn't add that part, either. She simply said, "Nan did her best."

"It's not likely that your grandmother would form such a close attachment to you and then pursue torturing other youth as some kind of hobby," Jack theorized. "But maybe her love for you made her more susceptible to those images. Like she couldn't shut off her visions because they triggered the power of her empathy."

Kate nodded. She liked any theory that featured Nan in a positive light.

Jack kept thinking aloud. "Where did she go, then? Would she have taken off to rescue the children?"

"No. She didn't leave of her own free will. She wouldn't have left the cabin like that, knowing I was on my way."

"Exactly."

"Someone took her."

"The same monster who stole the others."

Kate felt a wave of sickness crash over her. That meant there was a room somewhere rigged up to inflict agony on Nan. Kate remembered the anguished faces depicted in her grandmother's embroidery. Somewhere, Nan was suffering, too. Kate didn't know if it would be preferable to see the exact manner materialize in some weaving project. She blinked away tears, and the image of the scrawled message intruded on her thoughts. *It was supposed to be you.* How could that be? What importance had she, to make such an enemy? And more pressing: What torment was Nan enduring in her own place? She faltered slightly on her chair, just considering the possibilities.

Jack reached out to steady her. "We'll find her, Kate."

"I don't even know where we'd start."

"With the clues Nan left us." Jack said it as if it was obvious. "We've got to head back to her cottage. We need to take a closer look at those tapestries."

"Seriously?" Kate knew he was right, but her belly knotted at the thought of traipsing through the woods in the dark night, searching the shadows for the telltale yellow eyes of the hungry wolves.

And it wasn't just the wolves that terrified her. She remembered the absolute chill of her grandmother's cottage, the sensation that she was following the path of something truly evil. Kate knew she had to be brave for Nan's sake, but the dark, the wolves, and the terrible sense of dread all conspired to paralyze her with fear. In a small voice, she barely managed to whisper, "In the dark."

"No, not in the dark. It's too much of a risk with that battered ankle of yours. We'll move much quicker at dawn. Smarter to invest those hours in some solid sleep." He'd already started moving around the room as he spoke. As Kate watched, he took half the stuffed feed bags and piled them in the corner across from his sleeping alcove.

Kate felt torn—her vision blurred with exhaustion, her feet hurt, and her muscles burned. But she knew Nan might be trying to survive much worse.

Jack noticed her hesitation. "It's no help to your grandma if you collapse on the side of that blasted mountain," he told her. And then, more gruffly, "Besides, I can't have a sleepy little girl slowing me down. We'll sleep until the sun breaks—that's all."

Jack reached up and tugged a knit blanket from a hook on the wall. "This should warm you up. I'm sorry—I should have offered it earlier." Kate couldn't even form the words to tell him how silly it was for him to apologize to her after all his generosity. She just wrapped her shoulders in the woolen blanket, sank into the pile of cushions he had directed her to, and almost immediately slept.

CHAPTER 6

When she woke up in the dark, to the smell of burlap and wet earth, Kate initially believed she'd fallen asleep in someone's barn. The obscenely loud snoring she heard could only be that of livestock. Such sleeping arrangements wouldn't be such an oddity. Over the years, Kate had taken shelter wherever she'd found it—renting spare rooms, sleeping in a loft at the cooper's. Anyone who might make a bit of room for her in their home or at their table became Kate Hood's landlord.

She never lasted long in any one particular household. She had long ago stopped blaming herself. If she tried to be friendly, her hosts seemed to find her loud or immature. If she attempted to comport herself with more dignity, they called her aloof.

When Kate opened her eyes, she found herself in a dim, cellar-like place, stretched across a pile of stuffed burlap sacks. Her eyes flickered across her surroundings and all of the previous day's unexpected, unfortunate events came rushing back—the wolf pack, the disappearance of Nan, her terrible conversation with Dinah Flanders.

She remembered Jack Haricot and his kindness, right before the siren of his snore went off once more. Kate's hands instinctively flew up to her face and fluttered around her hair. She quickly rebraided her thick, chestnut curls and tried to rub the signs of sleep from her face. When her guilt kicked in, reminding her that she was fussing over her looks even as Nan remained missing, Kate talked herself through the shame.

He is a young man, after all, Kate reasoned. *He might be saintly, but he's also been totally deprived of human contact for the past year and a half. At least I might give him something to look at.* She recognized her own justification and bluster, though. Kate might not have had much practical experience with romance, but she knew enough to recognize the heat she felt in her face all the time, like a sunburn that wasn't quite showing yet. That meant she liked him.

She reached up and mussed her own braid. It wouldn't do to let herself get distracted. She worked quickly, piling up most of the cushions. She emptied one feed sack of stuffing and started packing necessities into it: a jug for water, candles. She found some jerky and wrapped it in a piece of cloth. Balanced on an overturned crate was a milk pail full of apples. Kate regarded them, weighing how many to pack, and then suddenly felt herself tumbling. She stood upright; her feet stayed cemented on the ground. Still, she felt herself pitch backward and drop through space. Kate blinked and found herself in a much different room.

She felt the cold steel of an iron bench beneath her and tried to leap up. That's when she noticed the metal cuffs around her wrists. They linked to the heavy chains fastened to the bench so that she could reach only to the scarred, wooden table directly in front of her. Her arms ached, weighed down the way they were. A wooden bowl of apples sat in the table's center, looking impossibly fresh, unbelievably shiny.

Kate could not explain how she knew about the apples. She could feel her belly clench in hunger and her head swim with dizziness. She glimpsed the brick walls that surrounded her. She couldn't see a door and sensed it was behind her. She shivered in the cold, damp, dim room. Shadows flickered on the walls, thrown by the wilting torches gripped by the wall sconces. She tried to keep track of all the details, filing them away for her escape. However, the shiny red globes kept pulling at her attention. She licked her lips with anticipation, imagining her teeth breaking into the waxy skin and tearing into the fruit, envisioning the juice running down her chin . . .

No, she tried to warn herself. *Don't.*

One apple would provide sustenance and gratification. The rest? Most contained a sleeping serum. Kate could somehow conjure up the sluggish feeling the sleep serum would trigger. She knew her limbs would grow impossibly heavy and a crushing feeling would settle on her chest. Her muscles would throb and burn and her lungs would claim to be pulverized. She'd feel as if she were drowning in despair as paralysis crept up her body. Kate-who-was-not-quite-Kate dreaded that sensation more than anything, perhaps even more so than the death she knew one of the apples held. Because one of the fruits had been injected with fatal poison. She knew that, too.

She reached for the first apple and peered at it, searching for telltale pinpricks. She checked a soft spot—was it natural? Could the bruising be the result of an injection? She tried to smell the fruit, but her stomach rumbled with demands. Her throat almost closed with panicked indecision.

"Which one?" a voice behind her cackled. "Which one will you choose?" Kate strained to turn, but the iron cuffs bound her arms. And the apples mesmerized her—she could not look away.

"You're not stealing from me, are you, Kate?"

She shook herself out of her reverie. Kate checked her wrists. Free. She recognized Jack's humble hiding place, so warm and inviting, compared to the grim room she had just witnessed. The apples in front of her looked like ordinary apples. Jack wasn't cackling. But his voice did sound menacing and cold.

"N-n-n-no!" she stammered and then cursed her nerves. But that just made her look guilty. "I just thought we'd need some supplies. I'm sorry—I didn't mean to presume." She started quickly emptying the bag, lining up each object on the rickety little table. Kate felt unsteady, distracted by the weird dream that must have spilled over from her sleep. She fumbled, trying to grasp on to the details that were quickly falling away from her, but also trying to smooth things over with her host.

"Aww, I'm just teasing you," Jack claimed, but Kate wasn't so sure. She thought she had just glimpsed a flash of the notorious Jack Haricot temper. Once again, she felt self-conscious.

Jack rose and stretched. He reached over her head, took a leather belt and purse from a shelf behind her, and fastened it around his waist. "It's not a lot, but if twenty-one ducats can spring us from some of the trouble, we'll be glad I brought my wallet."

"I can't take your money."

"Oh, I'm not offering it." Jack laughed, then added, "Yet. We can't leave it here—who knows who might discover this place when we're gone?"

"How?"

Jack only offered "You'd be surprised."

"But they haven't found it yet."

"They haven't found this one. This is the fourth hideout I've built." Jack looked around appreciatively. "Granted, it's only the second underground bunker and it's by far the best out of all the shelters, but the Shepherd's Grove enforcers are a savvy bunch. They've kept me moving."

The night before, Kate had found the outfitted hollow remarkable, marveling at Jack's woodworking skills and his gift for putting any discarded scrap to good use. Having learned that this was the fourth such home, Kate found his work even more awe-inspiring.

"How do you do it?" she asked. "How do you keep starting over each time?"

"Well, you know some about that."

Kate whirled around. She thought he was mocking her, but Jack's eyes were kind.

"It must have been tough," he continued, "trying to make it work at a different house every year or so. I figured you were some kind of rebel, getting booted by every adult who tried to care for you."

Kate remembered living with the seamstress and squinting by candlelight as she finished the mending she'd been ordered to do. She thought about old Agnes Davis, who'd served her chicken feed on a tin plate.

"That's not so. I tried to be the type of girl who deserved to stay." Kate's words stumbled. "They just didn't see it that way."

"I know," Jack said. "After I lost my mom, I understood better—that drifting feeling, how you must have been striving for a place somewhere. Listen, I understand why everyone got so angry with me. But I did what I thought was right—it wasn't my intention to bring trouble to the village. I remember expecting at least one of the town elders to step forward and say that."

"This is risky for you—traveling back to my grandmother's cottage." *Or traveling anywhere, actually,* Kate thought to herself.

"Maybe a little," Jack admitted. "But chances are, they'll all still be shut away in their houses, quivering in their boots and finding ways to blame their troubles on us." He nodded toward her ankle. "Are you worried about the return of your wolf pack?"

"That's why I'm bringing you along. To bite them."

"I doubt that will be necessary. I'm telling you, the circumstances dictated that attack more than the wolves did." Jack rechecked their supplies and laced his boots. "We'll move quickly and stay as low to the ground as possible." He checked to make sure Kate was listening. She nodded. "No paths. No sentimental dallying around your grandmother's cottage. We don't even look at those tapestries there—we grab them, pack them someplace safe, and get back to the bunker as quickly as possible."

Kate nodded even more vigorously.

"You feel okay?" Jack asked. "I mean, are you up to this today?"

"Of course I am. Let's get it done." Kate got to her feet and grabbed a satchel. She stood gazing at the round skylight leading up and out. "How does this work?"

"Usually, I just haul myself out." He flexed his arms.

Kate stared at Jack steadily. He tried, "I can boost you." She looked at him dubiously. "C'mon, we're practically family."

It took three tries before Kate could climb out of the underground warren and into the streaming sunlight. She sat in the shrubs off to the side and watched Jack expertly hoist himself up.

"Are you impressed?" he asked her as he glided elegantly out.

"Course not." She felt herself blushing again and hopped up. Then she quickly headed into the woods to duck under the cover of shade.

"Not so fast!" Jack called out. "Help me a bit here, will you?" He pushed the sheet of shale over his doorway and set about draping the blanket of moss over the hideaway's entrance. "Hopefully, we won't see anyone from town examining the ground so carefully. I thought this one was genius, but you uncovered it handily."

"It's a lovely piece of artistry."

"You're just that observant?"

"I was just that desperate." She watched as Jack stood up and stepped away from the bunker. Any trace of the entrance seemed to fade into the lush forest carpet.

After that, they made quick time up the mountain. Kate told herself she was moving more quickly because she was so well rested, but truthfully, Jack propelled her forward. She muscled through her sore ankle, but she couldn't escape the nagging regret. "I should have just brought the damn things with me," she mumbled. "That was me being lazy—I didn't wish to carry the blasted things."

"That was you being smart," Jack corrected. "What if you didn't find me and someone else found you instead? That would be dangerous enough, but imagine if you were also toting along a collection of creepy depictions of missing children. They'd throw you in the well and ask questions later."

Kate hiked along, somewhat mollified. She knew he was right. It had been the right call, even if it felt like every step up the mountain was another step backward. It felt different to climb up the mountain with Jack's reassuring footfalls behind her. *This must be what it would have felt like to bring a friend to visit Nan,* Kate thought wistfully to herself. Except for the obvious lack of Nan.

"We getting close?"

"You getting tired?"

"Not at all." She heard him pause. "The closer we get, though, the more careful we'll need to be."

Kate stopped in her tracks. "Why?"

Jack shrugged. "We could run into a trap. Or the villagers could have already headed up here last night, looking for answers themselves. It just never hurts to be careful."

As the vegetation grew thicker, Kate's paranoia increased as well. She worried most about the wolves. She couldn't picture the village enforcers, but the yellow fangs and glinting eyes of the pack were still fresh in her memory. She stepped warily, constantly scanning the vegetation for glimpses of her lupine enemies.

Kate didn't hear any howls or grumbling. Nor did she hear chipmunks chatter or foxes hiss. It took her a bit, but she realized that she didn't even hear the familiar melody of birdsong this deep in the woods—as if someone or something had turned over the forest like a jar and shaken loose all its contents.

When Kate spotted her grandmother's myrtle trees, the cold sense of emptiness that had greeted her yesterday returned. She motioned toward the landmarks, and Jack nodded in recognition. He raised one finger to his lips, but she knew enough not to speak.

Jack, who'd been hiking behind her, stepped forward then. She watched him head cautiously up the front path. *He resembles a deer or an elk*, she thought to herself. *He moves with such grace and silence.* She understood how he'd been able to move through the local woods without detection for so long.

Kate didn't trust herself to move as stealthily, but she couldn't just wait in the bushes either. She tried to step as soundlessly as Jack had, even following the path he'd taken, just in case. The house was as eerily still as the woods. While she might have missed the birdsong and the chatter of squirrels outside, the silence inside the house was far more disturbing.

She remembered what Jack had advised about dawdling and moved purposefully through the home's interior. Without speaking, the two of them developed a system. She would gently take down the tapestry: from its frame, from the wall, from what looked to be a table meant for stretching fabric. Then she'd carefully hand over each woven artwork to Jack. He would roll it up, arranging all of the rolls into a parcel he could carry safely under one arm.

In Nan's bedroom, Kate gathered the last of the tapestries and paused at the wrought iron bed. She indulged herself briefly and let one hand trace the top pillow. She knew if she lifted it to her face, she might smell her grandmother's scent—a mix of rosemary soap and firewood. The tapestries she'd come to gather shocked her, but Kate knew every stitch of embroidery on that pillow by heart. Gold and green thread flecked the willow tree's cascading limbs. A rosebush meandered around the willow's trunk.

Kate remembered when her parents had left. Six years old, she'd been almost inconsolable. She lay in bed for more than a week, tracing the threads on the pillow, inventing stories with joyful endings set in the sun-drenched meadow depicted in the scene. Nan had brought her bowls of soup and cups of tea and had sung her to sleep. She'd slept and dreamt of that tree, and picnicked with her parents under its shade. Then she'd wake up and the loss would stun her all over again. This morning had felt familiar in that way.

Jack looked back, wondering about the holdup. Kate braced herself for his impatient prodding. But he only reached out and gently shook the pillow out of its case. "We'll need something to wrap the tapestries in, right?" he asked. Kate watched as he turned the fabric inside out to keep the elaborate stitching safe. He tenderly slipped the case over the rolls of fabric he held in his hands. Then Jack beckoned her to hand over the last tapestry. As she did, tears sprang from her eyes.

"We'll be out of here in a few moments," Jack said gruffly. "Don't start weeping now. Once we're back out in the sunshine, I won't have time to calm you down."

Kate knew he was right. Besides, it was his kindness as much as her grief causing her to get choked up. She reminded herself that if she valued Jack's generosity, she needed to avoid testing it as much as possible.

So she said good-bye only in her head. To the wrought iron bed, to the stone fireplace with the carved mantel. To Nan's kettle. To her rocking chair. To the knit blankets hung from iron hooks on the door. She said good-bye to each of the things that seemed to stand for her grandmother, and then she felt them fall away as she let them go.

"Uh-oh." She heard Jack's quick intake of breath as they stepped through Nan's front door. The front garden was a sea of gray and sable fur. She counted more than two dozen canine backs tensed and ready to spring into action. It looked as if all the forest wolves had been summoned for a great assembly.

"So much for slipping out unnoticed," Jack murmured.

"Jack—" Kate's legs instinctively tensed, preparing to run.

"Steady, steady," he said. "We don't want to spook them."

"I feel like it should be a more mutual spooking, though," Kate murmured. "I'm spooked. You're spooked. Should we really allow the wolves to remain so comfortable?" As Kate muttered, she noticed a particular wolf staring at her. It licked its chops. "Did you just see that? That one is just mocking me."

She felt for the knife folded into the waist of her skirt. "No weapons," Jack warned sharply, and Kate winced. She didn't feel entirely keen about Jack calling all the shots. After all, she was the one with the teeth marks in her skin from the brawl the day before. And it was a different thing for a wide-shouldered giant-fighter to face down a pack of animals and declare "no weapons." Kate couldn't rely on the same muscles.

As her hand still hovered above the knife's handle, Jack spoke softly to her. "I'm telling you, Kate, you pull out that blade and it's all over for both of us. Eventually, someone might find smears of us on Nan's steps. Nothing else."

Kate clenched her jaw. Keeping her eyes on the pack, she nodded resolutely. "All right, then, they're all yours."

Jack exhaled slowly. He closed his eyes for the briefest of moments. *He's taking a moment for prayer,* she realized, and that did not reassure her at all. But then Jack stepped forward with the casual confidence of a boy accustomed to stepping into seas of wild animals. "Follow me," he encouraged her as he proceeded straight down the cobblestone walk in front of Nan's cottage.

"You're serious? That's the momentous and groundbreaking plan? Moseying on through?" Kate did her best to keep her voice calm and even, but in her head, her screams were as sharp as the knife she could feel pressing against her waist. The one she should be brandishing in her hand.

She forced her feet to move forward and keep the steady pace that Jack had set. About four steps in, she paused. More out of awe than fear. Jack simply sauntered casually through the wolves, the case of tapestries slung over his shoulder. His fingers even trailed along their fur, as if reaching out to pets rather than predators. The wolves mingled listlessly, baying here and there, sniffing at the hands that hung unthreateningly at Jack's side.

Kate mimicked his posture, his pace, and his very nature. Even when the yellow-eyed pack leader tensed her haunches, Kate gulped and kept walking. Jack took care to walk from one empty spot to another. He never squared off against a wolf or brushed too forcefully past. Kate watched carefully and continued to follow.

He passed through about the same time she reached the center of the congregation. She saw him reach the tree line and realized then that she was surrounded. Kate felt the living weight of the wolves around her, the breathing mass pressing from every angle. When she thought of how quickly they could overcome her, she choked in her dry throat. She imagined sinking to her knees, how they'd all take a piece of her. Unable to help herself, she let out a small whimper.

Panic leapt into Jack's eyes. For a second, she saw it. It surprised her that he would be so worried for her, a relative stranger. *Ahh—he's smart enough to know if these beasts turn on me, they'll get a taste for meat. The wolves will chase him down next,* she thought to herself. She told herself his concern wasn't personal.

After quickly composing himself, he nodded ever so slightly to her. *Keep going.* It took three nods before she could force her feet forward.

With every movement, she waited for the snarls to erupt and the teeth to gnash. The wolves settled, though. They continued to wander through the yard like depressed guests at a glum party.

When she finally caught up to Jack, Kate wanted to hug him with relief. She wanted to shout and possibly even stamp her feet. He immediately turned away, though. She would have thought he was angry, but he reached back to pull her along.

"Thank you," she said.

"Not yet." His words came softly and quickly, just like his footsteps. Kate turned slightly for one last glimpse of Nan's cottage, but Jack held her rigidly. "Don't look back," he warned. "They'll interpret it as a sign of fear."

Of course. Sometimes she felt so foolish. They were still in grave danger. All it would take was one wolf deciding on pursuit, and the rest would follow. She and Jack couldn't outrun them any more than they could have fought through the pack. Kate tried not to sigh. She aimed for the kind of bravery Jack seemed to display so effortlessly. She kept her gait steady, but listened closely for the sound of bounding paws or the sharp yips she knew often incited an attack.

The two of them walked almost a mile before they began to breathe more normally. Kate watched to see Jack's posture relax, his face seem to lose its stony mask of concentration.

"You think we're safe?" she asked.

He exhaled dramatically and grinned at her. "I think we're safe from wolves." He shoved her slightly. "No thanks to you, Princess Squealy."

"That wouldn't even qualify as a squeal," Kate defended herself. "I have a lung condition. It occasionally affects my breathing." But she laughed at her own lie and added, "I don't know what I worried for. Surely, they'd start with you."

"Oh, really? You think the *wolves* blame me for their giant troubles as well?"

"Course not." Kate smiled. "But you're the bigger piece of meat."

With the sun streaming through the canopy of trees and the light breeze at her shoulders, Kate felt the unfamiliar stretch of a smile on her lips. Jack looked looser about the shoulders, as if he, too, had put aside a burden for a bit. Kate knew there was still much to be accomplished, but in a matter of a few short hours, they had trekked up the mountain and retrieved Nan's tapestries. That was a start.

For a moment, they may have forgotten to be careful. They'd stopped ducking under trees and watching vigilantly for signs of travelers. Jack and Kate broke through the thistle branches of a mulberry tree, sort of celebrating—feeling brave to have faced down the mob of temperamental animals.

So they were very surprised to run straight up against a throng of angry men—Shepherd's Grove villagers. Among them was the cooper, the constable, and even the grizzled old drunk who called himself the town crier. When the villagers spotted Jack and Kate, the men raised the sticks and clubs gripped in their hands. Kate took stock of the whole collection of crude weapons at the pack's disposal. One man wielded an ax. One man waved a hammer.

"We've got them," the constable called over his shoulder. The would-be crier threw his head back and bayed, "The two suspects have been apprehended! I repeat: We have located the two suspects!" Kate noted his resemblance to a stray dog howling at the moon.

The mob increased by dozens. The men fanned out; Kate stepped closer to her only ally. Someone shoved her and spun her slightly so that she stood with her back against Jack's. She could feel the tremors of fear as they ran down his spine.

Then she saw the rope.

CHAPTER 7

"Kate, run!" Jack hissed. "Run as fast as you can."

"No chance." She spoke firmly. She meant she'd never leave him on his own to confront the rabid crowd who'd hunted him for over a year. But she also knew that fleeing would prove impossible. There were too many men waiting to chase her down. And how far could she get without Jack?

"Get back to Nan's cottage!" he ordered. "Take the tapestries and go." But the constable was already winding the thick rope around their waists. Jack began to strain, to leave her room to slip out.

"Stop. Jack—stop." She used her softest, calmest voice. "You have to keep calm." She recalled how steadily he had made his way through the wolf collective. If only he could carry himself with the same nonthreatening tranquility now. But Jack had been living in the wilderness for a while, Kate understood. He knew how to handle beasts. The villagers of Shepherd's Grove were less familiar predators. Kate reminded him, "We haven't done anything wrong; we mustn't act as if we have."

She couldn't see Jack, so she gazed into the eyes of Constable Sterling. She knew him, not to speak to really, but he brought his mending to the seamstress and occasionally dropped by the tavern to keep the peace. He'd never persecuted her, but he'd often let her know he was watching—just a village lawman, keeping the riffraff like her in line. Now he glowered as he cinched the rope more tightly.

"I'm sorry, Jack." Kate said it loudly, hoping the men around them were listening. "You were living such a peaceful existence and I involved you in this mess."

"Don't bother, beauty."

Of course, Jack would see through her contrived conversation.

"You don't need to tie us up," he told the constable as Sterling took the rope.

The town crier snorted. "Boy, we've had that rope reserved for you for months. And a cell in the village jail even longer."

Thomas Bane, the miller, held the ax. He folded his arms across his chest and declared, "That rope would serve just as well in a hanging." The crowd roared its approval, with fists jubilantly raising weapons in the air.

"Tom Bane, that's enough," Constable Sterling barked sharply, but the mob had already been incited. The men clamored to offer suggestions.

"Just weight them and toss them in the river."

"Nah, she'll float. Her kind don't sink, remember?"

"Not with that traitor weighing her down."

"Just leave them tied to a tree out here and let nature run its course."

"I say we draw and quarter them."

The constable spoke up again. "Gentlemen, please! We promised to deliver them to the king, and that's what we'll do." Kate almost gasped out loud. The king? What would the king want with her? Jack, maybe. But her?

One of the men checked to make sure the loop around them had pulled taut, and Kate cringed to feel his rough hands on her. She tried to focus on the feel of Jack's muscular back against her own. When the man checking the knots glared at her, Kate pressed her elbows into Jack's. He pressed back and she breathed deeply, reminding herself that she was not alone.

"Looks like they're all set," the rough-handed man called out to the constable.

"Are the suspects armed?" the constable asked.

Kate thought of how quickly the knife tucked in her waistband would slice through the rope. She remembered twisting it in the chest of the wolf that had attacked her. She felt Jack press his elbows to hers.

Jack volunteered, "I keep a dagger tucked in my boot. There's also a folding blade in a harness on my left shoulder. She's clean—I don't care for little girls carrying around weapons they can't handle. "

The constable nodded and set about retrieving Jack's knives. Miller Bane inserted himself in the scene once again. Kate saw that he was trying the constable's patience. She wondered how many volunteers the constable wished he could lock up in a cell beside the one reserved for her and Jack.

"You're not going to check her?" Bane asked in disbelief.

"You've got some real gentlemen serving with you, Constable," Jack observed.

"You keep your peace, Jack Haricot—"

"She's an innocent girl who simply got tangled up with a ruffian like me."

The constable looked dubiously toward her.

"Don't try to hoodwink the man, Jack." Kate narrowed her eyes at the man who'd suggested that she'd float if tossed into the river. "The truth is I don't need any of your earthly weapons." She curled her lip and pointed two fingers toward the man in her sights.

"YOW!" It had taken a few seconds for the man to realize that Kate had focused her attention on him, but as soon as he did, he sank to his knees, clutching at his head. "The pain, the pain! My God, have mercy! The witch has ensorcelled me!"

"You're not helping our cause any," Jack muttered. But he reconsidered as the men gathered around Kate's "victim." Even Tom Bane now stared at her fearfully. Constable Sterling was the only one who remained unruffled.

"You ought to listen to your beau," he said. "He knows a bit about inciting a crowd to riot."

Kate dared to ask, "You don't believe in the Uncommon?"

"Oh, I believe in them all right. But you seem fairly ordinary to me. Perhaps a bit naïve in underestimating how much trouble you've landed yourself in, but that's a common enough way to grow up quickly. The good lord knows there are worse things."

Kate noticed a cloud of regret pass over the constable's face. She wondered what worse things he had witnessed. And if they were somehow connected to Nan's disappearance.

"Move it along now, both of you." The constable took the pair of them roughly by their shoulders and shuffled them along. It took a few tries before Kate and Jack could coordinate their movements enough to sidle sideways without stumbling. They had made it mere steps away before the mob of men objected.

It was the one who had persuaded himself into a searing headache who led the outcry. "Are you mad?" he shouted. "You're going to present these heathens to the king?" Forgetting his blinding pain, he crooked an accusatory finger at the constable. "Owen Sterling, you've always leaned a bit toward the side of evil, but you've surely toppled this time."

"I'll take that under consideration," the constable replied wryly. He raised his voice and addressed the whole group. "Much appreciation for a productive morning! We've tracked down the subjects to whom the king wishes to speak."

"You do mean *suspects*?" Tom Bane interrupted yet again.

"Well, at this time, they are both. According to the will of His Highness."

"We're happy to accompany you to the palace," Bane said. It didn't sound like an offer so much as a threat, Kate thought as she watched the gathered men nod and puff out their chests.

"Not at all necessary," the constable demurred. "But I'll be sure to present your names there."

"We're not glory hounds, Sterling. You think that's what this is about?"

"I believe so, yes. And that's nothing to apologize for, gentlemen. It doesn't make the morning less early or the terrain less treacherous." Constable Sterling's voice dripped with condescension. Kate wondered how quickly she and Jack could sidestep away if the mob of men briefly distracted themselves by tearing their leader apart limb by limb.

Kate didn't see herself as an expert in working a crowd. After all, she had exactly one friend—the boy she was currently bound to. But the constable wasn't winning anyone over either, and he didn't even seem to understand the rage he was fanning with his every word. Kate made a quick wish that he would continue to act this way. It might just give Jack and her the opportunity to slip away. Then again, she and Jack might also find themselves trampled beneath the feet of the enraged search party.

She felt the slight nudge of Jack against her elbows again. "Keep calm there, Katie," he murmured.

"Sterling," Bane said, "we all have an interest in making sure these scoundrels face justice." The other men grumbled in assent.

It was, of all people, Jack who spoke next. "Maybe enlist the help of a few young ones?" he suggested to the constable. "Think of it as training some rookies. And it will appease the masses some." Kate could hardly believe him—giving advice about crowd control.

The only thing more surprising than Jack offering advice was hearing Constable Sterling take it. "Give me young Cooper, Buck Andrews Jr., and Little Peter," he barked out, and the boys stepped forward. When they looked at her fearfully, Kate remembered to glare ominously. She hoped they suspected a hex.

"That's very clever of him," Jack whispered in her ear. "Those three are sons of community elders."

"Why do you care?"

"Because they're also small. We could take them."

Kate looked back at the boys. She knew Jack was right. She turned to face the constable, who looked as if he was counting down the minutes until he could enjoy a cup of tea in his garden.

"Thank you," he addressed the men. "You helped out of the goodness of your heart and concern for your community. Please allow me to give these young men the opportunity to present your hard work to the king himself. Perhaps this experience will provide them a lesson on recklessness from their godforsaken peers."

Smart move, Constable Sterling, Kate thought. Even if he'd needed Jack's help to get there. The forest echoed with silence as the men considered their options. No one wanted to cut short the morning's excitement, but to insist on accompanying the constable and his young apprentices to the palace would be an act of pride that would be widely gossiped about in the village—a place that purported to value modesty above most things.

Chins began nodding. Thumbs slipped under suspenders. Hands gravitated toward back pockets. Pickaxes, hammers, and clubs finally lowered to rest on the ground. The constable's self-appointed deputy, Tom Bane, nodded to himself, and the others followed his lead. He called out, "We're going to double back. Make sure there's no others working with them."

"Don't hurt our friends!" Jack blurted. His false admission electrified the search party. The men picked up their pace, barely looking back at the small party facing the west side of the mountain.

"Are you finished with the theatrics, Haricot?" the constable muttered.

"Sir, I have no idea what you mean."

"Your friends?" Sterling snorted. "The ranks of your friends must have thinned a bit after you taunted a maleficent giant until he all but destroyed your home village."

"Really? Is that why no one came to my birthday party this year? And I thought it was the lack of proper refreshments. You're not going to thank me at all? I have the distinct feeling you didn't want the vigilantes sticking around for the whole day any more than I did."

"I do appreciate the peace and quiet. But I think their leave-taking serves you better. One of them might take matters into their own hands and inflict real violence—that concerned me. Not out of worry for either of you. But I didn't want to see a good man ruin his life."

"I didn't see a good man in the bunch," Jack retorted, and Kate looked nervously at the boys, whose fathers Jack had just insulted. She tried to nudge his elbows, but she couldn't be sure that Jack understood her message: *Calm down.*

Constable Sterling sighed. "Eventually, I hoped you'd learn that certain circumstances require a serious nature. Your solitary time in the woods apparently didn't give you the opportunity to cultivate that in yourself, Jack. I suggest you find it, quickly, today."

Sterling adjusted their ropes so that they were still bound, but not back-to-back, to make travel easier. Under the careful watch of their guards, they trekked on as a short parade.

Kate cleared her throat. "Why today in particular?" she asked, then added, "sir," hoping to show Sterling that she and Jack could certainly be rehabilitated by a reasonable elder willing to hear their side of things.

One of the younger boys scoffed, "As if you don't already know. You'll not beguile us, witch. We know your ways."

Jack announced, "Kate, I find you extremely beguiling." Kate found herself silently agreeing with the constable, wishing Jack would treat some subjects with solemnity.

Out loud, she chose to ignore the declaration and let out her frustration on the merchant's son. "Buck Andrews, you've never even taken the time to know my ways. Until this morning, you wouldn't have even taken the time to scrape me off your shoe."

"Not this morning," Buck sneered. "Until last night."

"What happened last night?" Kate hoped to gather more information about Nan. Maybe Buck or his powerful father had seen something.

"Don't you make a mockery of it!" a boy with blond curls called out shrilly. Kate recognized him as Paul Cooper; his father owned one of the largest plots of land in Shepherd's Grove. She'd never heard Paul speak up before. She knew the talk was that Mr. Cooper drank heavily and his family knew his hard hand. Paul's voice sounded as if he used it as little as possible.

She tried kindness. "I'm sorry. I wish I could help—"

"Enough lies! Why can't the prisoner be gagged, Constable?" Paul appeared to be pleading. Kate wanted to kick herself for the miscalculation. Someone as beaten down as Paul Cooper would never respond to kindness—he didn't trust it enough.

"Paul, this is part of investigating." Constable Sterling spoke firmly and carefully in a tone that told Kate he'd heard the same talk she had. Perhaps there had been nights when Sterling had needed to stop by the Cooper farm to calm its troubles. He continued speaking even as he prodded Jack and Kate forward, up a sudden steep incline. Kate lurched and stumbled. Only leaning into Jack helped her stay on her feet. "If we keep them talking, they might slip up," the constable continued with one last shove. Jack's body gave beside her. Or her body gave beside his. Either way, the bound pair tumbled to the suddenly even ground.

Kate looked up to see a massive granite castle stretching up toward the gray and cloudless sky. She'd seen it in paintings before but had never climbed all the way up the mountain to see it in its imperious glory. She'd never been summoned to do so.

The constable yanked her to her feet. Kate felt the weight of Jack follow. Sterling continued speaking over the hushed silence. "They might slip up and mention something, anything that might lead us to Her Royal Highness."

"Her Royal Highness?" Jack asked. Kate could sense him craning his neck to face his accuser head-on.

"Yes, Her Royal Highness!" young Paul Cooper cried. "Don't play us for fools." And then he asked in a voice drenched with anguish, "Where is Ella?"

Kate felt Jack press against her. And she felt a shudder, but she couldn't tell any more if it was she or Jack trembling.

"That's right." Constable Sterling glared down at them both. "The king's young daughter has gone missing. What have the two of you done with her?"

CHAPTER 8

"There's been a mistake—" Kate heard Jack's voice scurry and scram, like a mouse avoiding a cat's pouncing paw.

"You've made a few mistakes, Jack."

"Constable, that's right, but I would never . . ."

"You'd never what?" Paul Cooper demanded. "You'd never trade in your whole village for a handful of silver?"

"It wasn't like that!" Jack tensed with frustration.

"It was more than a handful," the constable offered wryly.

"You can't possibly think I'd kidnap a princess. For what? And why would Kate be involved? I mean, have you thought this through at all?"

"You'd kidnap her for ransom," Cooper's friend Little Peter piped up. "And you needed your Uncommon sweetheart to get past the palace security."

"I'm not actually Uncommon," Kate said mildly. Then she added, "Nor am I his sweetheart." She felt calm and steady and tried to radiate that steadiness toward Jack. "Could you please untie us?"

"Just walk forward," Sterling grumbled. "It's safer for you, anyway, if the guards see you tied up."

"Ella was beloved by her guards," Cooper explained.

"By more than her guards, it seems," Kate replied, sensing the unrequited affection in young Cooper's voice.

She heard the slap before she saw it coming. And then she realized she hadn't felt it because Jack had shifted himself in order to take the blow for her.

"What a gentleman, Cooper," Jack taunted. "Trying to hit a girl with her hands tied up. Your father would be proud."

"Damn you, Jack Haricot, I'll kill you, I swear to God!" Cooper raged. Little Peter and Buck Andrews held him back. A cloud of dust rose from their scuffling feet.

"Settle down. All of you," Sterling ordered. "We're not at the pub. We're about to enter the king's own home." The six of them made their way up the stone path toward the castle. Kate gazed down and tried to memorize each stone. They all looked expertly carved and fit together to depict a series of family crests. She inhaled and smelled the heavy scent of primrose and lilies. In some of the paintings she'd seen, mazes of hedges had surrounded the palace. Kate had heard it was possible to be lost for weeks in the green corridors.

Occasionally as they walked, Kate noticed a pair of freshly polished boots peeking out from tailored cuffs. Those were guards, she gathered, but she did not raise her eyes to look at anyone directly. She could only imagine what riffraff she and Jack looked like.

The doors to the palace stood taller than most homes in the village. Kate pictured the heavy wood planks used to build them—how many men must have been needed to carry them, what giant trees must have been felled for their sake. They glowed with a warm honey color, and Kate knew that some servant must spend hours polishing them with almond oil and lemon. Those doors mattered more to the kingdom than she did.

If the princess was missing, however, Kate knew the doors could not keep the inhabitants of the castle any safer than the humbler wood of her Nan's cottage. Nor the iron fence, the famous maze, or the formidable boots stationed at regular intervals.

When they reached the great doors, it took four men a full seven minutes to swing them open. An unseen trumpet heralded their arrival. As Kate stepped into the castle, she couldn't quiet down the surge of excitement, even though she wasn't there for a ball or a reception. She'd likely be interrogated, she knew. Forcefully. The king could do with her what he wished.

Their footfalls landed on the marble floors and echoed ominously. The three young men who had volunteered to accompany the constable on his mission fell back a number of paces, as if they didn't want to risk being associated with Kate and Jack. Kate glanced sideways and saw Constable Sterling's posture change slightly—his chest puffed out, his chin tipped up. He caught her looking at him and gazed almost kindly at her.

He knows very well we're not involved. Kate knew it as if she'd been taught it, the way she knew Nan's recipe for squab.

"Your Highness," the constable murmured as the invisible trumpet issued another brassy greeting.

It took several seconds for Kate to dare to raise her eyes. The man in front of her *looked* kingly. Wilhelm IV stood quite tall, with a narrow face framed with a thick, graying beard. Kate realized he was younger than she'd pictured. His eyes were a very vibrant blue, the kind you expected babies to have. The kind that usually faded. His hadn't.

King Wilhelm had dressed in some sort of wool uniform for the occasion. Kate had envisioned a crimson robe. She supposed the uniform counted as more practical. He did wear a sash of medals—mostly gold and bronze, pinned on brightly colored ribbons.

He spoke with a deep and melodious voice. Kate imagined it would carry across village squares during ceremonies and that it could shake chandeliers if it boomed in anger. "Sterling, these are they?"

"They are. Jack Haricot and Katherine Hood, Your Highness."

"And who are your young associates?"

"Well." The constable coughed and suddenly appeared flustered. "I believe you might remember young Cooper. These other two are sons of interested community elders."

"I do know young Master Cooper."

"Your Royal Highness." Paul Cooper bowed deeply.

"The three boys are dismissed."

"But, Your Highness, I believe I can be of service," Cooper unexpectedly spoke back. "Please allow me to help."

"You've done your part."

"Your Highness, I beg of you—"

The king merely raised an eyebrow slightly and Constable Sterling stepped forward, placing a hand on Cooper's shoulder. "Paul."

With a fast flourish, Paul Cooper whipped a dagger from his side holster and pointed it right at Jack's throat. "I can make them talk." In seconds, the king's guards had stepped from the shadows with swords drawn. Kate heard the glide of metal as the weapons left their scabbards. She saw Jack gulp and feared he would be nicked.

The king didn't blink. He seemed to measure Paul with his eyes, in tense and silent seconds. "Of course you can make them talk," he said. "I appreciate your service. But I have trained men here, should I need that kind of assistance." The king waved at the guards and their shining swords. "I assure you—we will send a courier to your home as soon as Ella arrives home safely. She will be honored to hear of your devotion."

Paul's face crumpled. Kate could practically hear him willing himself to remain composed in front of the king, in front of the father of the girl he loved.

"You've been a true help here, Paul," Constable Sterling offered. He nodded toward Buck and Little Peter, who stepped in to lead Paul away.

Kate could not turn to watch them go. But she jolted with a kick from one of them and then again when she heard the bang as one of the giant doors closed.

King Wilhelm sighed. "Was that necessary, Sterling?"

"Forgive me, sir. I hadn't considered the boy's affection for your daughter when I chose him. I defused one situation, only to ignite another."

"*Ignite* sounds rather dramatic. Right, Haricot? After all, it was a small knife."

"Was it, Your Highness?" Jack replied. "I only felt the sharpness of its blade."

King Wilhelm nodded in appreciation. He even looked momentarily amused. Then his face dropped again. Kate saw his grief in the hollows of his cheeks, his worry in the lines across his brow. "Her Royal Highness, my daughter, has gone missing. Her room, usually quite neat, was left in extreme disarray. Ella approaches life quite humbly. She had allowed me to assign her only one guard. We found the man slumped over, outside her door, drugged."

"You wouldn't be telling us this if you held us responsible," Kate blurted out.

"Ella is the daughter of the sovereign of this land," King Wilhelm declared. "Every dweller of my kingdom is responsible for her safety."

"Of course, Your Highness." Jack spoke as reverentially as she'd ever heard him. "I'm not wise enough to understand why you needed us dragged here under a cloud of suspicion, though."

"No, you are not." Constable Sterling issued a warning with his voice.

But the king held up his hand with all its rings winking in the light. "I consider it a fair question." The silence stretched to the cavernous room's peaked ceiling. "Provided it is indeed a question."

"Yes, sir."

"Well, you already live under a cloud of suspicion. You earned that. Yet you've been able to live undetected in the forests for the past year and a half. None of my own men have demonstrated that kind of stealth and resilience. And from what I remember, you are hungry. You were once willing to trade in your whole village for a fortune. This intrigued me."

The king's deep voice, which before had simmered, suddenly boiled over. "It is to both our detriment that I see only now how desperate my idea was. You haven't grown by much in wisdom. You still comport yourself with arrogance, disrespect, and selfishness. I had wished to offer you a second chance at the wealth that once slipped through your fingers. But I cannot trust you; this appears clearly to me now. So we will find another, regretfully. I can offer you a cell where you may wait and pray along with the rest of us for my daughter's safe return. If she does make it home, I will consider restoring you to your previous life of solitude in nature." Kate saw that the king spoke with true regret. His Highness might have seen a sliver of hope in the creative choice of hiring Jack Haricot, but the teenager's insolence had slammed the possibility shut.

Kate tried to do her part to prop that option back open. "And what about me? What do you offer me?" At first, Kate wasn't sure she had actually spoken out loud. None of the men reacted to the sound of her voice. She spoke louder and said, "Forgive me, Your Highness. I cannot curtsy because I'm tied with rope."

At that, King Wilhelm nodded to Sterling, who set to work unknotting Kate's bound hands and loosening the rope that held her to Jack. When the loop finally dropped to the floor, she exhaled with relief but then almost immediately felt oddly lonely.

Still, Kate curtsied as promised. Then she stood beside Jack, hoping to indicate that she didn't mind being lumped in with one who'd taunted the giant. As long as the king understood that she, too, had her price.

"You're the orphan." King Wilhelm might have been an archer with the accuracy with which he struck.

"My parents are long gone."

"Well, then I can offer you a home here. I won't promise you a title. You might know that Ella's mother died in childbirth, blessed heart. I remarried a widow with two daughters of her own. Ella and her stepsisters get along marvelously. We surely have room for a fourth daughter under this roof. You'd have yourself a family, if only you can find your stolen sister."

"Forgive me, Your Highness. That's a shockingly generous offer." And one designed to take aim at the bull's-eye on her heart, she knew. "But I do have kin of my own. My grandmother, who has also been kidnapped. I believe you know that. She has a powerful grip on magic, and those who stole her would not have dared to do so without your approval, tacit as it may have been."

Kate heard Constable Sterling suck in his breath. She could tell that he wished he could tie her back up, and that he'd follow Paul Cooper's advice to gag her as well. She saw her words inflict the barest ripple across the king's previously still face.

He told her, "I don't offer up my home to just anyone."

"I imagine you don't," Kate answered.

"And I do not entertain the Uncommon in my palace."

"Of course not, Your Highness." And then, because her words merely sat there like another set of silent guards, Kate added, "I am not Uncommon."

Kate swore she saw him glance away from her at that instant. But His Highness only declared, "What you are is quite young. You've allied yourself with an enemy of the State. You've spoken, if not disrespectfully, then certainly stridently to the king of this eternal dominion. And yet I believe that you are the only other person beneath this sky who shares my sense of desperation. Right now, you can't imagine claiming a seat at my table. My offer stands. Rescue my daughter. Use whatever resources you need and retrieve your grandmother at the same time. Would that bargain entice you?"

Kate didn't hesitate. "Yes, Your Highness." She heard Jack's breath catch. "May I humbly make one more appeal?" The king waved his hand to signal her to continue. "I'll need Jack Haricot."

"No one needs Jack Haricot," the king said.

She felt the air change to her immediate right as Jack held himself back from replying.

"I believe you underestimate him, as many do."

"Not so. I only underestimated Haricot once. I did not realize the utter devastation he could bring to my kingdom."

"Your Highness—" Kate heard Jack's voice catch, and was surprised when he did not go on.

Quickly, she jumped in. "Jack Haricot saved my life," she said. "More than once in the past day and a half. It is true he has a history of sacrificing the good of the community for his own personal greed." She felt, rather than saw, Jack slump slightly beside her. "He aims to make up for that. He is the only one I trust."

King Wilhelm took a long time to consider. During that time, Kate carefully studied her feet, tenderly leaning on her wounded ankle. Anything to avoid looking at Jack, whom she'd just called greedy and selfish in the middle of the king's Great Hall.

For his part, Jack was no longer slumping. Instead, he stood rigidly, as if his spine had been refortified with the same iron resolve that had fueled his eighteen-month sojourn under the cover of the deep woods. Kate recognized the resentment that emanated from that stature. At times, Nan had stood that way, too.

"Very well," the king said. "However, you must also bring along Constable Sterling." Kate turned to face the constable, but the man's eyes did not waver from their attentiveness toward the king. "You trust Haricot. I trust Sterling." The king tilted his silver-haired head. "We both have an immeasurable interest in the success of this mission. Sterling will accompany you and ensure that your efforts are not focused exclusively on your grandmother."

Jack spoke up. "Constable Sterling could barely control a rag-tag group of tradesmen and drunkards. Wouldn't one of your palace guards provide more expertise?"

Constable Sterling didn't flinch, but his upper lip curled into a wry smile. The king did not appear to register Jack's voice in the room. Kate waited through the silence, then said, "Very well, Your Highness. I am grateful for the additional help."

At that, the king nodded and spoke softly, more to himself than to anyone else. "There's a girl." He nodded to the guards lining the shadows of the Great Hall. "My men will provide hand-forged weaponry. We've packed a sack of gold coin." He glowered at Jack and added, "For the purpose of negotiation only. You also have some food and some skins to use as tarps. What else might help your work?"

Kate sucked in her breath at the sight of the gleaming weapons. The sharp blades and ax heads glimmered in the light. She judged from their slim points and polished glint that they'd be sharper than any household tools she'd previously handled—and far more effective than the lackluster knife still tucked into her waistband. Had she pulled the knife, she and Jack would never have stood a chance in this room, surrounded by armed guards. No more of a chance than Paul Cooper had. It occurred to Kate that the constable might have known she was armed. And Sterling had not even bothered to confront her.

"We'd like to visit the rooms of the princess." She tried to muster the right amount of authority into her voice, but she also took care to avoid sounding too forceful, lest the king consider her to be as disrespectful as Jack. "It might not help at all, but I wonder if we might get a sense of Ella."

King Wilhelm nodded. "Of course." He rang a bell in a distinct rhythm of chimes. In minutes, two girls swiftly glided in and curtsied to the king. They looked two or three years younger than Kate herself and wore fine calico dresses with white aprons. To her shock, they turned to curtsy to her and Jack, too. "Please show Miss Hood to Ella's quarters. Mr. Haricot might want to speak to our weapons expert."

"Actually—" Jack interjected. Kate heard the nervousness in his voice and understood. If they were separated, nothing guaranteed that Jack wouldn't end up in a dank dungeon, just as the king had suggested minutes earlier.

Kate nudged Jack's shin with her foot. "Jack understands it wouldn't be proper for a male to step into the sleeping quarters of the princess. He's happy to get a head start on the weapons training. He can pass whatever lessons he learns on to me."

The king bestowed a small smile on her. "Of course. You two have formed quite a partnership," Wilhelm observed as he strode from the Great Hall. The servants and guards curtsied and saluted, responding with mechanical precision to his movements.

She turned to Jack. "I'll be right back." He searched her face, so she added, "I promise."

"I know."

"Then why are you staring at me like that?"

"Who is this girl speaking so decisively to the king? She's not the same soaked goat of a girl who tumbled into my shelter last night." Kate couldn't speak. Her embarrassment surged for several separate reasons. "No, it's good." Jack laughed as he reassured her. "You're very impressive. I plan to learn some things from you, Kate Hood."

"Starting with diplomacy."

"Yes. Starting there. So please hurry back. I don't want to fail my first test and end up kneeling at the guillotine."

That image sped Kate on. She told the princess's maids-in-waiting to lead her forward.

"He's very handsome, miss," the one wearing her hair in braids offered as they scurried through the corridors of the castle.

"He's not my beau." Kate's voice stumbled over the statement.

"Whatever you say, miss." The one with a bun giggled.

"He's Jack Haricot."

Both girls gasped. The second one recovered more quickly. "Well, then, may the devil find him," she cursed.

Her braided partner hastened to add, "May the angels keep you safe, though."

Kate's heart sagged. *So that's what it's like to be Jack Haricot.*

Young girls beckoning the devil at the mention of his name, she thought. These maids-in-waiting didn't associate her with Jack completely, but Kate knew that some people would. Unless she could actually rescue the king's daughter, it was only a matter of time before people cursed the name Kate Hood as well.

CHAPTER 9

The three girls climbed a back staircase to reach Ella's wing of the castle. The stone steps coiled in a tight spiral and Kate felt slightly sick to her stomach as she pitched forward. She counted four flights before they reached a lonesome landing. Kate followed the princess's servants down a long hall lit by torches.

"Sort of spooky up here, isn't it?" she said.

The maids exchanged uneasy looks. The one with the braids admitted, "I suppose it is a bit gloomy."

"Beauty in gloom is still beauty," Kate murmured.

"What's that? I didn't catch that, miss."

"Just a saying my grandmother was fond of. She would say, *Beauty in gloom is still beauty.*"

"Would she, now? Miss Ella would appreciate that saying."

"Ella is beautiful, right?" Kate asked as they turned the corner.

"Of course."

"I mean if she weren't a princess, you'd still notice her in a crowd of others?"

The one wearing her hair in braids looked wistful. "Oh, yes, miss. You couldn't look away from Miss Ella. But she was—she *is*—kind as well. Most of the men in the palace vicinity have been cast under her spell."

"Louise is dramatic," Bun said flatly. "Miss Ella is very sweet and pretty. But it's not like she's one of the Uncommon." She chided her friend. "You must take care not to allow strangers to draw the wrong conclusion. Especially now that Miss Ella has gone missing."

"I didn't mean—"

"Of course not." Kate cut her off. "I would never believe that of the princess."

Louise looked relieved. "Margaret feels very protective of Ella. You couldn't imagine the terrible accusations her stepsisters made when they first moved into the palace."

"Really?" Kate said, wanting more information. "The girls don't get along? His Highness described it as such a loving family."

But Margaret's icy stare had already reached Louise, effectively shutting down that avenue of conversation. Kate knew that if she pressed, she risked the more guarded girl's turning on her. She shrugged, feigning a casual lack of interest. "I guess even the happiest of families suffer through their rough patches."

Margaret didn't fully buy her act. "This is the castle of His Royal Highness King Wilhelm IV. No one suffers here."

That wasn't entirely true, though—Kate could tell as much from looking around the expansive room housed in the castle's west turret. For one thing, she doubted the location of Ella's room counted as a coincidence, almost completely cut off from the regular traffic of the palace. Either Ella had resented her father's remarriage or whoever had designed the floor plans had deliberately cast her aside.

It looked comfortable. Having slept in more than one hayloft during her life, Kate brushed the lush quilted silk of the bedcover and understood that no expense had been spared in attending to the beauty sleep of the princess.

Still. She told herself that she was imagining it, but she recognized a certain loneliness in the room. Her various sleeping quarters, as comparatively sparse as they might be, had an identical mood. Kate recognized the melancholy present in the room of another motherless girl.

A portrait of Ella's mother sat framed on her bedside table. In it, her raven hair fell in ringlets around her face, and her eyes glimmered beneath slightly lowered lashes. Her head tipped back in laughter. The painting easily counted as the happiest thing in the room.

The rest of the décor could have been found in one of the palace's dozens of guest rooms: expensive fabrics, hand-carved furniture. Kate had never seen a gold chandelier hanging over a bed before, but she imagined that the sunlight would hit the thin wafers of crystal in just the right way so rainbows would filter across the bed of the princess in the morning. If only the heavy velvet curtains weren't drawn so firmly closed. Those curtains gave the impression that Ella hadn't let in the light for quite some time.

Kate checked behind the crimson drapes. She rolled up the rug and leaned against the floorboards, seeking a creaky spot that signaled a hollow. She knelt by the bed and slid her hand under the mattress.

Margaret coughed behind her. "I'm not quite sure what you're looking for."

"Nor am I," Kate answered as she sifted among the bed's several pillows. A worn rag doll tumbled out.

"Ella would be embarrassed. I'm not sure why she keeps that shabby doll. As you can see, she's not really one for sentiment."

Kate didn't even look up at Margaret. She traced the doll's embroidered mouth with her finger and looked into its button eyes. "Her mom probably sewed it." Kate tucked the doll tenderly behind a pillow. "It's lovely." She leveled her gaze at the two servant girls. "Where do the portraits of her father hang?"

"Well, in every other room of the house!" Louise blurted out before Margaret was able to reach down and clamp her hand over her arm. Then she spoke more carefully. "King Wilhelm loves his daughter dearly."

"Of course. That's why I'm here." Kate waited for Margaret to fill the room's silence.

"Miss Ella loves her father," the girl said.

"But maybe she's a bit angry with him?"

"I think *anger* is too strong a term."

"Who decided that Ella's room should be in the far turret?" When the gaze of both girls darted to the door, as if they hoped to escape, Kate knew she'd hit a sore point. "Please. Who made that decision?" She tried to coax out the truth with a softer voice. "I wouldn't press the matter if it weren't so important."

Louise moved to speak even as Margaret's viselike grip tightened around her wrist. She spoke up anyway. "Queen Cecilia—"

"Queen Cecilia thought Ella might enjoy her privacy," Margaret interrupted with what Kate understood was the official story.

But Louise would not allow herself to be silenced. "The girls couldn't get along." She ignored Margaret's hiss. "The queen's daughters moved in and made immediate demands. Anything Miss Ella had . . . she was—is—the apple of her father's eye, you see. Perhaps the girls felt threatened by that. Perhaps Queen Cecilia felt threatened by that, too."

Margaret looked around wildly and ran to shut the room's heavy door. "Trafficking in this kind of gossip is sure to earn us all a visit to the queen's dogs." Kate took stock of Margaret's pallor and understood that Her Highness's dogs were not a friendly breed of spaniel.

Kate turned the intricately cut crystal knob of a door in a corner and saw a vast closet. In it hung only a few dresses, the majority of which looked ragged and threadbare—certainly not the garb of a princess. She held up a hanger and wrinkled her nose. "Surely, Princess Ella and I don't share a seamstress?"

"Miss Ella is a beauty who doesn't need to dress luxuriously," Margaret hastily offered.

Louise spoke miserably, "The girls—they helped themselves to Miss Ella's finery."

"And let me guess—they moved into Ella's old quarters and drove her out into the guest quarters?" No one needed to answer Kate. The impersonal décor spoke volumes. "Why didn't the king step in?" Kate asked as she continued to search among the drapes of the velvet-canopied bed.

"I'm sure His Highness had other matters to attend to." Margaret spoke primly.

"It's one thing to have your clothes stolen and be shoved off into a lonely tower, but did the girls ever strike Ella?" Kate dropped her voice to ask. "Did the queen ever hurt her?"

"No, miss." Both servant girls spoke at the same time, in the solemn voices of maids who knew they could be executed should they answer otherwise.

It was no matter. Kate knew the pain of being rejected and hidden away. She knew that the lonely nights Ella had spent missing her own mother counted as harm enough. She understood the envy the sad princess must have felt, watching Cecilia and her daughters. "His Highness described the room as in shambles. Have you neatened it?"

"We did, miss," Margaret said flatly.

Louise hastened to add, "On the queen's orders."

Kate knew asking for further explanation would prove fruitless. "What did you need to straighten?"

"The bed was a mess, with sheets tangled on the floor—"

"Her Highness always fixes her own bed, directly after rising."

"One set of drapes had been pulled down. And the glass on her mother's portrait had been shattered."

For a few moments, none of the girls spoke. Kate broke the silence first. "His Highness also mentioned an incapacitated guard."

"Yes. John Boulder usually kept watch through the night. The morning sentry found him unconscious, with the distinctive foam of belladonna poisoning at the corners of his mouth."

"Would Ella have run away?" *I would have*, Kate felt like adding. *No matter how comfy the silk brocaded bed looked, I wouldn't live out this nightmare.*

"Miss Ella took her duties as princess seriously. Her mother trained her to do so. She wouldn't have fled and let some interlopers serve the people in her place."

Margaret sounded so certain. Then Louise added, "Miss Ella would never have caused any harm to John Boulder."

Kate nodded. That made sense. Besides, she had searched every corner of the tower room and, aside from the doll, had found not a single item that revealed any aspect of Ella's personality. Time ticked away, she knew. She could spend days wandering the castle's hundred rooms and in that time, Ella and her Nan might slip farther and farther away.

"Thank you." Kate looked each servant girl in the eye and then curtsied to them both. "I know that you risked something to speak so candidly to me. I now know how loved Ella is, to inspire such loyalty."

"Thank you, Miss Kate." Margaret's look had softened a bit and she sounded sincere. "Please let us lead you back to the Great Hall."

On the way down, Kate took the steep stairs two at once. This time, she left the servant girls practically panting as they tried to keep up with her. She felt the sad weight of the tower bearing down on her and ran faster. Two flights down, she heard the metallic clang of weapons practice and quickened her steps again. Kate could not have predicted the amount of relief she would feel at the prospect of seeing Jack again.

She wondered if Princess Ella had a friend like that. Perhaps Paul Cooper? Of course, Jack was not devoted to her in the way that Paul was to his princess. Obviously. Kate felt embarrassed to even make the comparison. But having experienced the tower's oppressive loneliness for less than an hour, she could not help hoping that Ella had something in her life that quickened her step and alleviated her grief ever so slightly.

"Jack!" She practically shouted his name. He did not look up until he'd successfully blocked the advance of one of the king's expert swordsmen. When Jack pushed aside the heavy metal mask protecting his face, she saw the light in his eyes dance.

"I'm learning to be even more formidable, Kate."

"Oh, but is that possible?"

Kate looked back to see the servant girls making the last round on the spiral staircase. She noticed the glower descend on their faces and remembered their harsh words about Jack earlier. She breathed deeply and stepped forward. "Miss Margaret and Miss Louise, please meet my friend Jack Haricot. The two of us are going to do whatever we can to bring Princess Ella home safely."

Jack bowed in his own charming and theatric way. "Ladies, the honor is mine, I'm sure."

"I am sure that the honor *is* yours," Margaret said haughtily.

But Louise stepped forward at least and ducked her head in a cursory curtsy. "Good to meet you, Mr. Haricot."

"Did you find anything useful, Miss Hood?" King Wilhelm's voice boomed across the Great Hall. Kate saw that a beautiful but severe woman now accompanied the king. Queen Cecilia stood almost as tall as her husband. She had a high forehead and a long neck draped in strands of jewels. Her height and the length of her neck gave the appearance that her whole self was arching, like the spine of a provoked cat.

"I feel a stronger sense of your daughter, Your Highness. Surely, that will be useful in our search."

"This is the girl?" Queen Cecilia may have married the king only three years before, but she had achieved an imperious tone usually reserved for one born to the crown.

Kate mustered a curtsy. "Your Highness."

"My husband feels the desperation of a frantic father. Most subjects would be too loyal to capitalize on that."

"I believe his loyal subjects would do whatever possible to help, Your Highness. Jack and I will do our best to bring the princess home."

"Good luck to you, then." Kate heard the thinnest thread of a threat woven through the queen's words. As she glanced around the room, she saw that no one else had picked up on it.

"We'll leave before the hour's up, Your Highness," Jack told the king, then paused before adding deferentially, "I thank you for the weapons training. Truly."

"Before you leave, you'll both be suited with armor. And you'll each choose a steed from my stable."

"Again, we thank you."

"There's one more thing," Kate burst out. Jack turned to her incredulously. She understood his confusion. He was trotting out his best manners and she was standing in King Wilhelm's castle, making demands. But she barreled through. "I'd like to speak to Queen Cecilia's daughters."

She watched the queen steel herself even further, but before Her Highness could refuse, Kate added, "I've heard that the girls were so very close. Princess Ella may have confided in them. Of course, I don't want to intrude. Your daughters must be distraught at the loss of their beloved companion, but perhaps they might have picked up on some tiny detail that someone else—someone with a less sisterly bond—might have overlooked. Perhaps it would help them work through their sorrow to feel like they were contributing to Princess Ella's homecoming."

King Wilhelm clasped his hands together and nodded. "Of course, of course. I should have thought of it. I'm sorry, darling. I didn't mean to overlook the girls."

The queen stared icily at Kate. Kate watched her eyes shift, the gears turn in her regal head. She couldn't refuse the request. She couldn't correct Kate's version of her daughters' relationship with the princess. Her hesitation told Kate that the girls were not as practiced as she. If Queen Cecilia and her daughters had orchestrated the kidnapping or even allowed themselves to be bought off by a greater evil, Kate might be able to shake something loose.

"Don't give it a second thought, dear. Of course, Ella has occupied your mind. How thoughtful of you, Miss Hood." Cecilia then beamed her sharp voice toward Margaret and Louise. "Fetch my daughters, please. Let them know they have the opportunity to speak to the searchers charged with finding their dear sister."

"We're hardly searchers, Your Highness," Jack offered guilelessly.

"Well, you are something, indeed. I can barely think of another name." Cecilia answered Jack but stared down Kate. However, Kate's attention had already shifted. The hall echoed with the sound of giggles and scampering feet.

The girls rounded the last turn of the spiral staircase before remembering to go somber with grief. Kate watched the queen's face flash with annoyance, and hoped to see King Wilhelm's brow furrow at the fakery. The sisters might be empty cisterns of information, she knew. But at least she could help expose them to Ella's father.

Ella's stepsisters did not count as ugly. They were lanky girls who had not yet grown into their mother's height. Their pale blue eyes looked like watered-down versions of the queen's ice chips. Whereas Cecilia's hair and arched brows were jet-black against her pale skin, her daughters were both strawberry blond. Kate found herself wondering if Cecilia colored her hair to achieve the striking contrast of her looks. The girls looked more ordinarily pretty.

"Allow me to present my daughters, Calista and Cassandra." As Kate bent her knees, Cecilia added, "The girls are merely citizens. It is not customary to curtsy to them."

"Good day," the slightly taller of the two offered, sending a warm look in Jack's direction. She elbowed her sister, who giggled and promptly clamped her hand over her mouth to stifle the sound. Neither appeared distraught, or even capable of putting on a half-decent show of it.

"I'm so sorry about your sister," Kate offered.

The girls swung their blue-eyed gaze up and then at each other in confusion.

"Your stepsister, Ella," Kate clarified.

"Of course," the taller one said. No giggles this time. Just an obviously rehearsed line. "We hope Ella returns as quickly as possible. We'll make it our life's work to find her."

Kate noticed Queen Cecilia grimace at this, but again, none of the men in the room seemed to pick up on the strangeness. Jack might have spent the day learning weaponry, but Kate would need to school him on the cautious listening of women.

"Had you noticed anything strange about Princess Ella of late?" she asked the sisters.

"Of late?" The shorter girl's voice quivered with what Kate could swear was held-back laughter.

The other stepsister let out a discernible snicker. "Princess Ella has always been a bit strange." With that, a full-out cackle escaped the shorter girl's lips. Kate glanced at the king, who stared blankly, seemingly oblivious to the way his wife's daughters mocked his Ella.

"Maybe she sensed some kind of danger?" Kate pressed.

"Perhaps the princess felt uneasy or had the sensation that some-one was watching her?"

"The only people who ever watched Ella were the guards paid to do so." The taller girl spat out the words, eliciting another round of hissing laughter from her sister. Shocked, Kate turned to Jack, only to see him looking as blank and unruffled as King Wilhelm. Couldn't either of them hear the two girls laughing like jackals about the missing princess?

But then, Kate noticed the smug look on Cecilia's face. The queen's lips curled into a sneer. Kate had seen this look on the faces of the girls who refused to invite her into their lunch circle, who mocked her for her sloppily sewn dresses. She remembered the cold eyes of the mothers who forbade their daughters from playing with her.

Women didn't need to be Uncommon to treat each other evilly, Kate knew. But still, there was something strange happening. King Wilhelm couldn't have fallen so in love with his new bride that he would tolerate such flagrant disrespect from her daughters. And Jack wasn't dense.

Kate didn't know if the queen was ordinarily evil or exceptionally evil. It was the latter that could have brought the chill she still remembered from Nan's cottage and created the empty void that had overcome Ella's room.

An unexpected voice broke the spell. Constable Sterling had faded to the background once he had agreed to accompany Jack and Kate, but now he stepped forward and touched her elbow lightly, murmuring, "Let it go." Kate realized that the constable saw and heard Cecilia as clearly as she herself did. She stared.

Sterling nodded. Kate understood without asking that they would discuss Cecilia's strange power of camouflage afterward. The queen's smile turned sly.

"Wise counsel." Even her voice weaseled. Cassandra and Calista bent their heads toward each other, whispering. Their shoulders shook with silent laughter. Kate felt the steady presence of Jack beside her. And now Sterling also propping her up.

She no longer believed Ella would want to be returned to her place in her father's palace, and for that, Kate felt a new kinship with the princess. She needed to rescue her along with Nan.

Kate stood up as straight as she could and faced the dazed king and his wretched wife. "Your Highness, I so appreciate the time you've taken. It's clear Ella's sisters have been struck silly with grief and fear. Perhaps if Jack and I achieve our mission, it may help make your family right again."

Cecilia nodded serenely. King Wilhelm reached for her hand. "As you can see," he said, "Ella is so very loved. Godspeed, Miss Hood. Mr. Haricot. Sterling. Feel free to arm yourselves at the iron forge on the property. And please allow my coachman to escort you to the stables. Your choice, I insist."

Suddenly, Louise lunged forward from her place at the steps. "Miss! Miss!"

"Why, Louise. Control yourself." A warning bell rang in Queen Cecilia's voice.

"I just wanted to thank you for taking the time to learn about Princess Ella." The servant girl leaned forward to kiss Kate on both cheeks. As she bent toward her, she whispered, "Miss Ella loved her horse Weston. She spent hours at the stall, grooming him."

Kate grasped the chapped hands of the maid. "I'm so grateful for the tour." Because the queen was listening intently, she added, "And to have heard from you and Margaret how happy Her Highness was in this home." Kate hoped the lie would deflect Cecilia's wrath for a bit.

"Perhaps you, too, could find happiness in these walls," King Wilhelm proclaimed grandly, like a man with no inkling of the rot corroding his home from inside. "Remember the terms of our agreement, Miss Hood. Ella is my greatest treasure, but I would make room for another daughter with her return. And reward Mr. Haricot handsomely as well."

"Of course, Your Highness." They stood at the soaring front doors. Kate considered their weight again. She imagined what it might feel like to live in a home with doors too heavy to push open herself. Ella must have felt like a prisoner.

"Sterling, I expect regular reports."

"Certainly, Your Highness."

Footmen yanked on iron chains to pull open the doors. Kate stopped herself from darting directly out into the sunlight. King Wilhelm's palace reached to the sky, but it still felt too small when brimming with the malice of Cecilia and her daughters. Only outside the castle did Kate finally feel she could breathe. She turned to curtsy one last time to the king.

The door was already shutting, though. She hoped Wilhelm understood her gratitude. And she hoped his help counted as legitimate, and that his intentions could be trusted.

Kate, Jack, and Sterling followed the coachman toward the stables. Once there, she tried to hide her awe. Kate had slept in more than a few stables, but she'd never had access to the kind of plush accommodations that housed the king's horses. She counted more than twenty stalls. They even *smelled* good.

"His Highness issued strict instructions: You're to choose any horse, each of you. They are all sound beasts, strong and fleet of foot. Well cared for. They'll serve you well."

"We'll continue your high level of care," Jack offered sympathetically. He patted the coachman's shoulder, but the man only shrugged him off.

"We don't keep pets here," the coachman replied shortly.

Constable Sterling strode ahead of the group. "I'll take the gray dappled gelding, with much appreciation to King Wilhelm."

"Excellent, sir." The coachman nodded to a groom, who immediately set about saddling the gray horse.

Jack paced back and forth before settling on a mare the color of rich mahogany. He patted her haunches and tipped his hat. "Much obliged."

Kate finally spoke up. "I would like to ride Weston, please."

The coachman stopped and turned. "That's Princess Ella's horse!"

"They're not pets, right?"

"Of course." He paused. "Right away." Kate noticed that the coachman didn't pass on the task of saddling Weston. Instead, he crossed the stable to a stall right in the middle of the line. He lovingly tousled the mane of the fawn-colored beauty and set about oiling the saddle and checking the horse's hooves.

As the coachman readied the horse, Kate found herself looking deeply into Weston's eyes, wishing he could speak to her. *The things your mistress must have confided in you,* she thought to herself. But Weston only looked at her steadily. Ella's secrets were safe with him. While Kate stared and attempted to manufacture a spiritual connection with the horse, the coachman sighed quietly and stroked the horse's back.

"Never mind," Kate said abruptly.

"Miss?"

"I don't like the look of this horse," she announced, meeting the gaze of the coachman. "And Princess Ella will want to come home to find her horse so well cared for."

The servant allowed himself the slightest of smiles. "Very well, then. Might I recommend Lucius, the sable horse in the very last stall? He is our fastest."

"Thank you."

As soon as the coachman headed out of the stall, Kate quickly combed through the fresh hay on the floor. She didn't know what she was expecting—she found no trace of Ella. She patted the knotty pine walls and the horse itself. Then she spotted Weston's food trough.

Making sure the coachman was busy readying the new horse, Kate sifted through the oats left at the bottom of the trough, her fingers closing around a familiarly textured sheet. It felt like burlap, but when Kate brought it out to the light, she gasped. Before she could even call his name, Jack rushed to her side. He was there to see her unroll the fabric and expose a tapestry, as ornate as the pieces found in her grandmother's cottage. This one depicted a grieved version of Ella, sitting on an ash pile in the corner of a shadowy cell. Her hands were shackled and the same silvery thread depicted a loop of chains connecting her to the wall by the waist. Kate noticed the princess's hands looked red and swollen, as if she'd been soaking them for hours in lye. Kate knew the look of hands like those—they were hands worn down by hard labor.

Ella's eyes did not look sewn. They looked like bottomless reservoirs of sadness. And that was frightening. But sewn across the top, in the familiar jagged embroidery, were two words that inspired more fear.

You're next.

CHAPTER 10

Jack let out a low whistle and stood quickly.

"Let's go, Kate," he said. He reached out for the scroll and she handed it over, dumbly. "We can't really speak freely on King Wilhelm's land," Jack murmured as he put Ella's tapestry into the sack with the others. "Let's just concentrate on getting on the road first."

Kate felt grateful for Jack's decisiveness. Otherwise, she might have sunk down right there in the fresh and fragrant hay. She had tried to convince herself that Ella had simply run away. The tapestry—its haunting image and its menacing message—carried with it a reminder of the large evil their little group faced. That she herself faced—Kate knew that, when the time came, she would not allow herself to hide behind Jack and Sterling.

The coachman and his grooms had lined up the horses. Lucius looked as powerful as promised. Jack helped her up into the saddle and loaded up their packs. Constable Sterling looked over with concern as he mounted his horse. "Something I should know?"

"No." Jack's denial was firm and immediate.

"Yes," Kate overrode him. "But let's get some miles under our belts first." She gazed down at the coachman and his crew. "We thank you for everything."

"We all want to help bring the princess home."

"Does she spend a great deal of time here? In the stables?"

The coachman nodded. "Aye. She does. She and Weston have a bond. Her Highness has a way with animals." He hesitated, then added, "Sometimes, animals are kinder than people." His quiet comment gave Kate the distinct impression that Ella had confided in someone. Perhaps him. Or perhaps the coachman had merely been listening as the princess confided in Weston.

Kate nodded. "True. Again, thank you for your help."

"Yes. Thank you," Jack echoed. Constable Sterling tipped his hat.

As their trio galloped off, Kate couldn't help but listen for hoofbeats thundering behind them. It was difficult to imagine

King Wilhelm sending Kate and Jack off unaccompanied. But of course he hadn't. Constable Sterling rode alongside them.

Kate, Jack, and Sterling rode for two hours straight before slowing to stop. When Jack slowed down and edged his horse toward a clearing beside the trail, Kate exhaled with relief. She wasn't used to riding and her whole body ached from the constant jostling. At the same, she wondered if they should just keep going. They'd already wasted enough time.

"Good a place as any?" Jack asked. He hopped off and led his horse a few feet to a nearby stream. Then he helped Kate down and led Lucius toward the water. Sterling followed suit. Jack said, "Circumstances aside, it's a bit freeing to ride out in the open. For the first time in almost two years no one's pursuing me."

Sterling looked up sharply. "I wouldn't count on that."

"Something you'd like to share, Constable?" Jack challenged. Kate hoped she wouldn't need to constantly broker a peace between them. *We already have an enemy,* she wished to remind them.

"Nothing definite." Sterling glared at Jack. "And don't mistake my prudence. I stand loyal to King Wilhelm."

Jack threw up his hands in mock surrender. "Aye, aye, Captain." He knelt down to start a fire. "You sure sound devoted."

Sterling searched for the right words. "I have reservations."

Kate could see the lawman struggling. "You were speaking to me. In the palace earlier. Without actually speaking out loud."

Sterling looked pointedly toward Jack. "I'm not so sure about that."

Kate only said, "I am." She wouldn't start keeping secrets from her one friend. So she asked the constable in front of him, straightaway, "Are you one of the Uncommon?"

That got Jack's attention.

"I'm not like your Nan," Sterling answered. "But I appreciate her power. And I believe that one doesn't necessarily have to be Uncommon to employ that kind of gift."

"How did Cecilia manage to bewitch Jack and the king but not you?"

"What are you talking about—bewitch?" Jack asked. "The woman was attractive, sure, but I wouldn't call her *bewitching*."

"How would you know? You couldn't hear half of what she had to say," Kate retorted, and then described the strange deafness Jack and King Wilhelm had displayed. "But Sterling heard all of it." She gazed at him in wonder. "And you even spoke to me, but not aloud. I heard your voice in my mind."

"We understood each other," Sterling explained simply. "I wouldn't characterize Cecilia's conduct as Uncommon. Classic witch behavior, perhaps, but that's not the same thing."

"It's not?" Jack sounded dubious.

"Not really. Would you like to explain, Kate?"

Kate shook her head. "I'm no expert."

Sterling looked slightly exasperated, but he continued. "What we call Uncommon are merely human beings who are able, through training or inheritance, to tap into advanced clairvoyant activity through concentration and practice. From the outside, the abilities of the Uncommon look magical. Really it's more as if the Uncommon work a set of muscles the rest of humanity have left unexercised. There are times, I'm sure, that you have feelings—gut instincts about future happenings."

"I'd wake some mornings and just know that it was time to move on and build another bunker."

"And because you trusted your instincts, you evaded capture."

Jack grinned. "Well, that and the complete incompetence of the law."

"Wonderful," Sterling said drily. "I would imagine that more and more, you began to follow your own gut. That's usually how it goes, when people live in isolation." Jack considered that and nodded. "That compounds the situation with the Uncommon—they display these strange abilities and are pushed to the outskirts of society. Then, while living on the outskirts, they grow even more reliant on their own instincts. They pass those traditions on to their children. Or grandchildren."

"And what about witches?"

"Aside from extraordinary ability, there's not actually a lot of common ground there. Witches are not fully human. They are not born as infants. They do not grow the way we do. They are the result of adult humans making transactions with dark forces. In exchange for power and supernatural abilities, they offer space in their bodies to demonic forces. As the human hosts age and become weaker, the demon component claims more territory in the body."

"That's why the more powerful witches are old ladies?" Jack asked. Kate assumed he was thinking of Nan.

"Sometimes, they do look like old ladies. But sometimes, one of the powers they cultivate is a resistance to aging."

"So how old do you think Cecilia really is?"

"Not so old. Young enough to have had those teenage daughters, at least. In part, that's why I don't believe she's responsible for this latest spate of evil. It would take an exceedingly powerful creature to drag off King Wilhelm's daughter." Sterling looked to Kate. "Not to mention your Nan."

"Because her grandmother is one of the Uncommon?"

Sterling stayed silent and let Kate handle the question. She breathed deeply and did not immediately answer.

Jack continued to build up the fire now crackling before them. Kate watched the flames lick the narrow pieces of kindling and felt the welcome warmth against her face. She stared into the fire's glowing center and suddenly felt herself fall, as if she might have tumbled off her perch on the log and kept falling. Kate could not force her eyes from the flames until suddenly, there were no flames.

The canopy of trees above her had been replaced with a bare, granite ceiling. No more fresh air, cool breeze, or carpet of grass. There were only brick walls and an iron bench. And the iron bench was growing uncomfortably warm.

She turned toward Jack, but the boy beside her was not Jack. He looked much younger, with the chubby cheeks of a toddler. When the boy reached out to grip her arm, she noticed their limbs were roughly the same length. How could she be so much smaller? Her legs dangled from the bench as she shifted. She swung her feet and was surprised to notice they wore white socks and black buckle shoes. Her legs were bare and felt chapped.

"Hot," the boy whimpered.

She managed to squeak, "Hot," in agreement. She wished she could add, "Lost. Afraid." The fat tears on the boy's cheeks made her chest ache—she wanted so badly to console him. She held his hand and tugged him to the floor. The floor felt like clay and it, too, was warm, but less so than the bench. The floor didn't hurt, although she swore she felt it growing warmer.

She and the boy scurried to the corner of the tiny room, near a thick metal door with a grated window. She pointed and the boy nodded excitedly. He crouched on all fours so that she could climb onto his back. Steady, steady. Shakily, she stood upright and strained to reach the barred opening. She felt the boy shift and shot out a hand to steady herself. The door scorched her palm. She fell backward.

She tried to shake the hurt out of her hand, but her fingers had already blistered. Her palm looked seared—as if she'd pressed it into a skillet on the stove. She sobbed, and the boy patted her head to console her. He splayed open her raw fingers and lightly kissed the center of her hand. She felt momentarily comforted.

But then they heard the noise. Someone smacking her lips. A sinister voice called out, "It won't be long now. Don't reach for that door again, dearie. I don't care for a crispy skin on my meat!" And then she heard that awful cackle. Even as the room's temperature ratcheted up another few degrees, that cackle chilled her to the bone.

They were roasting alive . . .

"Kate?" She blinked to find Jack studying her. The campfire now roared. "You okay? You're awful close to those flames—you'd best scoot back. I hope you don't think I'm judging your grandmother—"

"No," Kate said. She could not explain to Jack and Sterling what she had just seen, where she had been. She herself had no idea. So she spoke about what she felt sure of. "Yes," she said. "My grandmother is one of the Uncommon."

Jack kept a close eye on her. "It makes sense that a witch would take on one of the Uncommon. Imagine the jealousy. Someone who traded in a piece of herself for a power that the Uncommon just pass down among themselves."

"That's a fair point," Sterling said to Jack, and looked somewhat impressed.

Kate was still lost in the confusion of her strange waking nightmare. *I just have to find Nan,* she reminded herself. *Nan will know what these visions are. She'll show me how to make them stop.*

"But what about Ella?" Jack asked Sterling. "Surely, she's not Uncommon?"

"She could be," Sterling pointed out. "She's isolated and rather smart. Popular with the servants we met today, which suggests a high level of empathy. She might not be genetically Uncommon, but she might have developed skills out of desperation. Perhaps she recognized her stepmother for what she was and tried to find some answers in common folklore."

"Well, that seems to have worked out well for her, hasn't it?"

"Jack! It's not her fault she was kidnapped." Kate remembered the desolate feeling of the iron shackles around her wrist, the burn of the locked, hot door.

"No. But it's not ours, either. Forgive me if I don't get worked up over the very sad life of a princess."

"Hers *is* a very sad life."

"I'm sure. With only her servants to talk to and her purebred horse. The poor girl has to sit alone in her comfortable rooms and try to force down the food a cook prepares for her. Maybe her silken sheets occasionally get scratchy."

Kate understood his resentment, but she could not feel it, not after what she'd seen. "She's not so different from us, Jack," she said.

"Think of where you've been sleeping each night for the past few years. Think of the nights you've gone to bed hungry. I've had to dig out rooms not much larger than graves. The people who bow down to Ella have hunted me down. Relentlessly. Like a dog. And suddenly, I'm free to move about, aboveground even, because I'm willing to risk my life to rescue her. I assure you—Princess Ella is very different from you and me." He shoved one last piece of kindling into the roaring fire. "I'll do what I have to do, because this is my ticket out of living in cellars. And because you're a good kid, and if you have a chance to get your Nan back . . . well, I see that as worth my time and effort. But some princess? Crying into her velvet pillow? I reserve my sympathy for people who deserve it."

"So you're just here for the financial gain, then?" Constable Sterling countered.

Kate felt hollowed out and weary of all the pain in the world. *Why invite more of it?* she thought.

"It's a valid reason," she interjected, saying it so she wouldn't have to listen to Jack make excuses.

"It's not just gold." Jack looked hard at both of them. "And it wasn't just gold last time, either."

"You mean the giant?" Kate asked, and then felt like slapping herself. Of course he'd meant the giant.

But Jack just shrugged and said, "It's good to move freely again. I never aimed to be the town's villain."

"It wouldn't be so terrible to become the fellow who saved a princess instead of the kid who taunted the giant," Sterling summed up.

Jack nodded even as Kate pointed out, "Well, you do need a princess for that. So don't spurn Ella just yet." She rummaged around in the pack King Wilhelm's men had put together for them and cut off a few hunks of meat from a coil of sausage. Kate grimaced and hoped Jack and Sterling didn't notice. She could not imagine eating meat just then, no matter how badly her body needed sustenance. "So maybe Cecilia didn't orchestrate the kidnapping, but do you think she was in on it?"

"I think she benefits. As do her daughters." Jack sounded very sure of this.

Kate nodded in agreement, and Sterling added, "The queen probably has the ability to send ahead word about us. Whoever we're facing will know we're coming."

"And who are we facing? Any inkling?"

Sterling spoke carefully. "I think your Nan must be the key."

"Can you think of anyone who wanted to harm your grandmother?" Jack asked gently.

Kate remembered her weekly treks through the forest, and Nan's refusal to move into the village, despite the growing impracticality of her cottage. "She had many enemies—the whole village, really. I never knew why. She shielded me from all that. I always had the sense it was connected to my parents. Constable Sterling, did you know my parents? They would be just about your age."

"Your parents?" Sterling looked away into the woods. Kate got the distinct impression he was avoiding the subject.

"My father's name was Joseph. He married Rebecca Weathers. Nan has said she was quite beautiful."

"I'm sorry—"

"She had a number of suitors, Nan told me. Even though the family was rumored to be Uncommon, she still caught the eye of several young men. She chose my father, who was just an apprentice traveling through. Joseph Hood. He was an iron forger."

"I'm sorry." The constable spoke more firmly. "I don't remember."

"Well, surely you remember their disappearance?" Jack studied Sterling carefully, then prompted Kate to speak more. "They just vanished one day, right?"

"Not exactly. They left. I have a blurry memory of them packing, and my grandmother's tears as she begged them to stay. They sat me down to tell me they had a duty to serve and that I was to be good for Nan until they returned." She smiled wryly. "So I've been trying to be good for the past decade."

Sterling still refused to look straight at her. "I'm sure your parents would be proud of you." He stood up and brushed the dead leaves and dust off himself. "It's getting dark. This was a good place to stop, Jack. I suggest we hunker down and get some rest."

"It seems early to sleep." *And too early to stop talking,* Kate wanted to add.

"The sooner we sleep, the earlier start we can get in the morning."

Kate stared at Jack, willing him to somehow stall and get Sterling talking again. "Anyone want any more to eat?" he offered. It was all he could come up with in the circumstances.

"We'd best take care with provisions," Sterling said decisively, and Kate almost cried in frustration. She looked to Jack again. He stood up as well.

"We should review a few things now, before nightfall." Jack crossed over to his horse and retrieved the burlap sack. "If the three of us look at these together, maybe it'll jog something—some memory—I don't know. These tapestries count as our only actual clues. As constable, you must know more about the people in them than Kate and I do. And the backdrop of each looks unique—you know, like a real place. We should all be on the lookout and know what it is we're searching for."

Constable Sterling hesitated, but what could he say? Kate saw him searching for a way out, but there was none. Jack had made a perfectly reasonable request.

"Of course," Sterling said, facing them with a smile Kate would swear was plastered on his face.

"Great. Let's take a look." Jack spread the embroidered pieces on a flat piece of moss beneath a massive oak.

Laid out together, side by side, the tapestries created a terrifying exhibit. And it scared Kate more to examine them out in the woods, with just a few trees for shelter. Her skin prickled. It was as if something evil had swooped down and settled in one of the trees above them.

"There's a distinct pattern to the bricks here." Sterling traced the threads with his fingers. "You can see the same design on the wall in this scene and this one." He leaned down to look even closer. "I want you both to see these leaves." He pointed out a trail of vines that snaked along the wall in the tapestry depicting the girl with the shaved head. "We need to look out for similar vegetation. And the construction: It's all the same brickwork, but these are several dungeons. That has to mean a large palace—on the scale of Wilhelm's. Or it's a building dedicated to holding captives. Maybe a prison." Sterling tilted his head. "Your grandmother wove these?"

"Yes. I mean, I think so. That's what it looked like since a few were still hung from looms in her cottage. They were scattered all over. Some finished, others in progress. But I never actually saw her working on them." Kate heard herself, but could not stop babbling. It didn't matter that Sterling seemed to have landed on their side somehow. He was still the king's man and she knew that linking the tapestries to Nan could incriminate her.

"Had you seen them before? Or other tapestries?"

"No. Nan occasionally sewed linens—the pillowcase, for example—but never anything so . . . vivid."

Jack dutifully spread out the pillowcase so that Sterling could see the much simpler sampler for comparison.

"And when had you last visited?"

"The week before."

"You're sure?" the constable pressed. Kate nodded. "Absolutely certain?"

"Yes. I made—make—a weekly trip up to her cottage with Nan's groceries. I had no occasion to make a special trip earlier in the week. So it had been seven days."

Sterling nodded at the collection of elaborate embroideries. "That's a great deal for anyone to accomplish in seven days. But imagine your Nan in particular—picture her squinting in the candlelight or how her fingers must have ached."

Jack connected the dots. "Something was driving her. Desperately."

The constable kept examining the evidence. "Would you say these works display your Nan's typical skills?"

Kate found the question silly. He had the pillowcase right there. Obviously, Nan could stitch a scene, but nothing as stunning as the tapestries. She looked up at Sterling with annoyance. "They clearly do not." She felt hope surge in her chest, then crash again in confusion. "No one else was staying there. It was just Nan. So although I'd like to believe she was hosting some expert weaver with a devastating imagination, I would have known if she had a guest. For one, she would have instructed me to purchase extra provisions."

"Calm down, Katie. He's just trying to help."

Kate bristled visibly at Jack's words. She refused to meet his eyes and acknowledge his cheap betrayal. Sterling rushed to pacify her.

"I'm sorry," he said, in a manner that appeared genuine. "I don't mean to treat this as a game. But it's important that you draw your own conclusion. Physically, we've all accepted that your grandmother must have sewn these scenes. But the work isn't typical of her abilities, and the time frame in which she completed them is unrealistic."

Kate looked steadily at them both and remained silent.

"Don't you see, Kate?" Jack burst out. "Your Nan must have been taken over. She channeled some kind of evil, but the evil didn't originate with her."

Kate nodded warily. "That makes the most sense to me. I thought so when I first saw them—when we found them. But I still didn't want to share them, just in case . . ." She trailed off.

"Good." Sterling nodded to himself. "Then we're all thinking along the same lines. And we all understand that your grandmother needs rescuing, just like any other innocent victim. These tapestries don't change that."

"Yes." Kate almost thanked him, but silenced herself.

"Okay, then."

She heard something tender in his voice and leapt for it. "Constable Sterling, you *must* remember my parents."

"I wish I could help you." Sterling's voice sounded raw enough that Kate believed him. "But maybe I can help bring your grandmother home. That's something." He looked back toward the woods, as if the answer could be found in the trees.

Kate felt a gentle hand at her back. Jack. "Let's turn in for tonight," he said quietly. "Check the horses and set up under that canopy over there. We won't be visible from the trail." Kate leaned back against him ever so slightly. "Okay? Does that sound right? We'll all get some sleep. Maybe take another fresh look at these in the morning."

Neither Sterling nor Kate nodded. They just drifted to the horses and set about the chores that went along with caring for an animal. They took off the saddles and patted flanks. They checked to make sure the vegetation on the ground was safe for grazing. Kate pulled out the heavy woolen blankets from the packs. Each horse got one, as did each rider. The night was warm and clear, so no one moved to pitch the canvas tent that had been rolled into Kate's pack.

Kate settled down first. She felt her chest constrict, wondering where Jack would lie down. She let herself imagine for the briefest instant what it would be like to sleep with her head curled against him. His flannel shirt would feel soft against her cheek. She might even be able to hear his heartbeat.

Out of the corner of her eye, she watched the constable lay out his blanket several feet to her right. He rested his head on his pack and lay with his face turned toward the sky. She heard Jack's scuffing footsteps and how they stopped between her and Sterling.

"Fire's still smoldering. I'll wait until it's out."

"Sounds good, Jack. Good work today," the constable told him. Kate pretended to sleep, taking deep, even breaths. She heard Jack linger and then a branch crack. She figured he'd turned back to the fire.

Eventually, she leveled off into a deep, dreamless sleep. She drew the woolen blanket close around her shoulders. When Jack shook her awake, he tugged on that blanket. "Kate, wake up." He whispered it so close that it tickled her ear. He sounded desperate. "Listen, I've got a bad feeling about Sterling. Please, Kate. I want us to go."

CHAPTER 11

"You want us to go where?" Kate asked, propping herself up on her elbows.

"Shhhhhhh! I just think it's for the best. Let's just move along, the two of us. We don't need Sterling."

It took Kate a few moments to clear her head of the cobwebs of sleep. She fought to sit up and rubbed her eyes. The thick darkness prevented her from seeing Jack's face clearly. He loomed over her as a blank, shadowy figure. She could see how rigidly he held himself. She could feel the tension radiating off his body. Beyond Jack, Kate could see the crouched mound of the sleeping constable. Her eyelids still felt heavy. "Jack, go back to sleep. We'll talk about it in the morning."

"We might not get a chance to speak alone. I don't have time to explain everything. He could wake. Please just trust me. Kate—"

"Okay. Okay." Kate threw the blanket from her shoulders and leapt to her feet. The action woke up the rest of her senses. She could hear Jack's heavy, adrenaline-laced breath, Sterling's steady snores. Dark shapes came into sharper focus and she moved quickly and deliberately.

Jack reached out and grabbed her upper arm. "Really? You're sure?"

If she hadn't been so aware of her every slight noise, Kate might have snorted. "No, I'm not sure. But I trust you."

He nodded vigorously. "Right, right. Okay, then."

There wasn't a lot to pack. They'd all taken care to organize their sacks before resting, just in case.

Kate grabbed her bag and took up Lucius's reins. The horse protested the sudden wake-up call with sluggish feet and a snappish tail. She patted his side. "Sorry, friend," she murmured. Then she looked to Jack. "Which way?"

In answer, he stepped ahead of her with his horse to forge a path in the night.

As they filed off, Kate looked back to Constable Sterling. The depth of grief she felt surprised her. She didn't think of herself as fond of him. But it had felt safe for a few hours to have an adult take charge. The sting of tears crept behind her eyes. She ducked her head. Even in the dark, she wouldn't risk Jack seeing her.

Jack picked his way carefully through the forest. It was a tricky thing to expect a horse to walk into unfamiliar territory in the pitch-black. They made slow progress, Jack and Kate each watching the trail closely. They frequently patted the horses, trying to reassure the nervous creatures, who'd been pampered just the previous night. Kate knew they were open targets for anyone charged with hunting them down. More than once, they passed a leafy glen that looked like an ideal spot to resettle, but she let Jack lead on. She understood that they needed to gain some real distance if they really meant to leave Sterling behind.

"Should we mount and ride?" she whispered at one point, but Jack shook his head emphatically.

"Too dangerous. The horses are skittish enough, and we don't know what kind of ground is ahead of us."

"Smart creatures, these horses," Kate muttered before she could stop herself.

"What's that supposed to mean?"

Immediately, Kate wished she'd kept her mouth shut. What was the point of following Jack blindly just to then whine like a bratty little sister?

"I'm sorry, Jack. But I just don't understand."

"You didn't get a strange feeling from the man?" Jack's voice rose with incredulity. He immediately corrected himself to a whisper. "Kate, when we first met him, he bound us with rope."

"On orders from the king. And that was theater basically, designed to get us to Wilhelm as desperate criminals. That way, we'd help him."

"The men in that mob, who demanded the right to drown us in the river—they didn't consider it theater. It could have gone very wrong, you know. They could have overpowered Sterling. He could have been straightforward and simply asked us. Most people would serve when asked."

"We're not like most people. Would you really have served when asked?"

Jack walked several feet before answering. "Probably not. But I deserved to make my own decision on fair terms. Wilhelm let me choose between searching for his daughter or rotting in a dungeon. That's not really a just choice."

Kate nodded. She could see his point. "But that was King Wilhelm. Do you think Sterling knew from the start that we weren't to be charged? And if he did, do you blame him? I mean, do you really expect him to be more loyal to us than to the king?"

"I am." Jack turned to face her, but the tiny words tumbled out so quickly she didn't quite understand. He tried again. "I am more loyal to us than to the king." Kate felt her chest and neck flush with warmth.

He had just said the word *us* as if they counted as a kingdom of two. That was something Kate wanted to believe. But Jack was Jack the Giant Killer. He hadn't exactly earned a reputation for loyalty.

"Katie, I won't let anything happen to you," he said now.

Kate thought of the desolate prisoners depicted in Nan's tapestries. She remembered Queen Cecilia's icy stare and could still feel the deep chill of the air in her Nan's abandoned cottage. She thought back to the messages that had targeted her. She doubted that anyone, even Jack, could kill whatever giant evil they were facing. It was so dark she could barely see Lucius in front of her. She felt weary and scared and wished to believe in something. So she simply nodded up at him and said, "All right, then."

They trekked along in silence while the sky lightened. Sterling would wake up and find them gone. At first, he might dismiss their absence as a bad decision made by stupid kids. He might think they'd been fueled by young love. *Are you sure that isn't the case?* Kate could practically hear Nan drolly question.

Sterling would know they hadn't been kidnapped, because he'd see they took the horses. Kate knew he would come after them. Not because he necessarily cared so deeply. The king had given his orders, and Sterling was a man who followed orders.

She and Jack had precious little time to put some distance between them.

"You really didn't think he cared about us at all?" Kate asked as they navigated one particularly tricky turn.

"Who? Sterling?" Jack looked back at her. "Does it really matter?" He must have seen from her face that it did matter. Jack kept leading his horse forward, but as he did, he told her, "You know, Kate, I never really knew my pa. He made his living as a tinker. He traveled through villages fixing things, but he left my mom broken. So I know what it's like to look to any grown man who speaks kindly to you and wish for his last name."

Jack seemed to think through his next words carefully. "Most men don't go around collecting other people's children to care for. Sterling might not be the kind of evil we're searching out. He might just see an opportunity. We're orphans. That makes us disposable to men like Sterling and Wilhelm." Jack stopped and stretched. "I think it's safe to stop for a few minutes and rest. And the horses probably need water."

Kate tugged on Lucius's reins. She set her pack next to a tall birch and rubbed her tired shoulders. "You just seem so certain about him—Sterling."

"No, the point is that I'm not certain at all. But I'm absolutely sure about one thing—last night, he lied right to our faces. There's no way he couldn't have known your parents. And the whole time, he sat there studying the tapestries—talking about plants and bricks. As if those people hadn't been kidnapped on his watch. Someone doing his job, who lived and breathed to solve the mystery of those disappearances, would have been all over those tapestries. Which means one of two scenarios: Either Sterling doesn't care or he already knows exactly what's become of those vanished victims. If that's the case, he was walking us right into some kind of trap."

"Maybe he just feels guilty. I know he lied about my parents. He couldn't even look straight at me. But that doesn't necessarily mean something sinister. All my life, people have avoided talking to me about my parents. Even Nan."

"Do you want to turn back?"

Kate considered it. She pictured storming an evil castle, caught between two dubious characters. Sneaking through dark corridors with suspicious Jack and resentful Sterling. For a flash, she considered heading out on her own. The drama that men and boys created tired her. But she glanced at Jack, at the way his curly hair looked lighter as dawn approached. The dimple that ducked into his cheek slayed her. He'd called them a kingdom of two.

"No, I don't want to turn back." She took a deep breath. "How long can we rest?"

"Another few minutes? I'd like to put down a few more miles

between us before sunrise." They watered the horses, gulped down some breakfast themselves. "We can saddle up now."

Kate's thighs ached from all the riding the day before. She'd prefer to keep leading Lucius by the reins as if he were a particularly calm dog. But she reminded herself of the tapestries. Who knew what kind of torment Nan was experiencing? Surely, Kate could handle a few strained muscles.

As they prepared their horses, the air felt different between her and Jack. They'd barely acknowledged the strange web of feeling between them, but there was no time to sift through all that right then. Kate threw back her shoulders and hopped up onto Lucius before Jack could offer to boost her.

For a moment, Kate closed her eyes. "Nan, if you are close enough to hear me—we're out here, searching for you. If you could give us some inkling, some sign of where you are . . ." She trailed off when she felt the horse shift.

Jack peered up at her. "Casting spells, Katie?"

"Just trying to tap into my Uncommon ancestry."

"Well, good. We need any advantage we can get." He swung his bag over his shoulder and mounted his horse. "I say we keep following this stream north. It might make it easier for Sterling to track us, but any castle as isolated as the one in the tapestries would need a water source close by. Sound good?"

"Yes, it makes sense."

"But does it feel right?"

"I'm not one of them, Jack. Those are skills you need to cultivate. I've spent my whole life trying to avoid accidentally practicing."

Jack shrugged and kept forging ahead. Kate looked down at the saddle and smiled to herself. She would find Nan. And as soon as her grandmother felt up to it, Kate would ask her to start educating her. Maybe it was time to start embracing her heritage.

Kate felt the sun on her neck and realized it was now morning. Lucius picked up his pace as if he was finally accepting that the new day had arrived. She would find Nan today. They would spend the evening cleaning up her cottage and she would catch her grandmother up on everything that had happened, including King Wilhelm's offer of a family, her burgeoning friendship with Jack Haricot, and the idea that it had the potential to grow into something even more unexpected.

"Hey, do you smell something awful?"

Trust Jack Haricot to break into her romantic thoughts with such an unromantic question. But as Kate rode farther, she did smell it. Once she'd lived in a shed of a hunter and his family, took room and board in exchange for chores. She'd had to scrub the blood off his weapons and clothes. From that, she could recognize the smell of fear and death anywhere. And this smell was ten times as strong, easily. She felt her stomach twist—and had to grasp her horse's mane to keep from vomiting.

"Ugghh. What is that, Jack?"

But Jack was occupied, trying to guide his stumbling horse. "I don't know what—" He grumbled as the horse sank to its knees.

"Jack—move away from the stream. Now! Leave the horse if you have to." Kate snapped the reins and veered Lucius toward the left, off the trail into the leafy vegetation. She prodded him faster, checked the ground for poisonous plants, and leapt off the saddle. Then she raced back to Jack, who still struggled waterside with his steed.

The noxious odor threatened to overpower her. Kate swayed with dizziness. One peek over the bank of the stream confirmed her theory. The water frothed green. She choked back sick. "Get away from the water," she repeated. She stretched out her hand. "Leave the horse if you must."

"Are you mad? I'm not leaving my horse." Jack looked at her as if he didn't recognize her. The horse's eyes almost rolled back in its head before fixing on Kate. She could swear it was pleading. Jack stood there tugging, as if he could pull the impressively built beast to safety.

"It's no use, Jack," Kate whispered.

"I'm not leaving my horse, Kate," Jack repeated through gritted teeth.

Kate stooped down and tugged along with him. The horse barely moved an inch. "Jack—"

"Just leave us, then."

Kate felt like screaming in frustration, but she knew that would just startle the fallen horse further and make the situation even more dangerous. She looked helplessly around—there was no one and nothing to help them. So she crouched farther down and tugged, right along with Jack. Kate felt her muscles wail and her jaw ache from clenching. She released all of her frustration and fear into the effort and suddenly felt herself falling back as the horse's iron-shod hooves clobbered over her.

The three of them—Jack, Kate, and the sick horse—tumbled backward in a tangle of limbs. The horse recovered first and hobbled to a standing position. When it bolted into the trees behind them, Kate shut her eyes, relieved to see the animal was not injured. Then she groaned. Her body throbbed complaints through every nerve. Kate felt Jack's hands under her arms and she, too, slid toward the forest's deeper cover of foliage. He kept dragging her until the dense air thinned and they could both breathe again. Then he lowered her to the ground.

"Jack Haricot, you are a madman."

"I am? The world hasn't seen strength like that . . . well, since a naïve little kid managed to defeat a giant."

Kate rubbed her sore arms. "Well, I suppose you didn't need my help, then?" She slowly rose to her feet.

"Your help? Kate, that was all you—you pretty much just lifted a horse." Jack regarded her carefully.

"Don't look at me like that. Like I'm an aberration of nature."

"Has that happened before?"

"What? No. Nothing happened. It was just you and me—working together. Our efforts laced with a healthy dose of desperation. Are the horses all right?" Kate still couldn't move quickly or surely.

Jack checked on the animals, who stamped the ground and whinnied in agitation. He examined their legs and held each animal's snout as he scrutinized their eyes and mouths. "They're nervous, but seem fine enough. How do you feel?"

She felt shaky. Her throat burned from whatever gas they'd all inhaled. Her body felt overstretched. "Fine," Kate told him. "I feel fine. And you?"

Jack coughed and she heard a rattle in his chest. His eyes looked red-rimmed and bloodshot. "Oh, I'm okay. I feel okay. We must have wandered near some poisonous plants. That's all."

Kate knew he'd seen the water. They both had. "Jack, it's obviously the river."

"Nah, it can't be the river. We've been drinking from it for days now."

"It's dammed up somehow up here. There's something in the water. It's green and foaming." She moved closer to him so that she could really see him. He didn't seem ill, just worn out, like she felt.

"Green and foaming? Let me see—"

"Jack, no!" Kate grabbed his arm. She'd used up all of her reserves of strength, though. She could barely keep her fingers clasped around his wrist. She tried to stay as calm as possible and make sure her voice sounded fierce and commanding. "Jack, you've been bewitched." He still pulled back toward the water. She felt his resistance and knew she could not let go. "The water's poisoned, Jack. That's why your horse fell. It would have died after lying there much longer. You and I would have died. That smell—it signals an evil presence." Kate concentrated every last drop of strength into one final yank on Jack's arm. "Jack, you'll die if you go back to that river."

He snapped back toward her. Kate still felt that presence, watching them from the trees. She could swear she heard it sigh with disappointment in the breeze. Jack stared at her, dumbstruck, then rubbed at his eyes. "Kate, I need to sit down. But I need to see that water. I just need to know. We should make sure."

"Let's just have you sit down." She stepped under his arm so that he could lean on her. She expected to collapse any minute but knew he just might crawl over her. She understood enough about enchantment to know its pull could be that strong. Kate managed to half walk, half drag Jack over to the two horses.

She worked quickly, unbuckling his belt. Jack sighed. "Katie, I can't believe I'm saying this, but I'm not so sure this is the proper time—"

"Oh, for heaven's sake, shut up, Jack Haricot." She whipped off his belt and used the leather strap to lash Jack to Lucius's stirrup. Lucius looked down at her as if she was punishing him, too. But her horse had been exposed for the least amount of time. Kate figured he would be more resistant to any kind of spell, even if it was directed to animals as well as humans.

Jack looked ridiculous. She'd used his back belt loop, so he sat there slightly hanging from the saddle's stirrup. He gazed up at her, deflated and helpless—a marionette that had crumpled to the ground. "What is the meaning of this, Katherine Hood?" She almost laughed out loud at Jack's outrage.

"Just relax for a few minutes, please." Kate allowed herself a little chuckle. "You look like a scolded child."

"This isn't what I expected you were meaning at all." Jack pouted.

Kate was sure she went scarlet with embarrassment. She turned away and busied herself with searching through their packs. She was sure King Wilhelm's cook had packed emergency canteens. Once she found one, she poured some water into the cooking pot and held it up for the horses to drink.

Kate realized her mistake the moment Lucius began slurping indelicately. The water immediately drenched Kate's shirt and soaked her shoes. Resigned, she held the pot up for Jack's horse to drink. Jack himself made no comment, sitting dazedly at Lucius's feet.

What a sight we must be, Kate thought to herself. *The pair the king sent to rescue his daughter.* Jack looked drugged and she had no idea how to draw him out of his stupor. She'd just doomed herself to cold and wet out of a concern that the horses might be thirsty. Kate couldn't help questioning the decision to give Sterling the slip. *We're just kids, after all. Who are we to take on such a charge?*

Jack gazed balefully up at her. She grabbed a tin cup and dunked it, then knelt beside him. "Drink this, please," she commanded, hoping it might dilute some of the poison that had obviously overcome his senses. "Jack, you must get yourself right. Really. You seem to think I know what I'm doing, but I have absolutely no clue. You're the expert in evading capture and defeating dangerous enemies, right? I'm basically a washerwoman. I'd thought it very clever of me to enlist your help. That way, I could tag along and sail in on the winds of your bravery. Jack, please. King Wilhelm made you feel small and inconsequential. King or not, he had no right to do that. And he tricked us, you see—elevating me. Making me feel like some kind of authority. Maybe he meant to cause some trouble between us. Or maybe I just got a bit too big for my britches. The truth is, I don't know even know how to ride a horse correctly. Just now, I gave the horses water out of a pot. I might as well have served them a cup of tea.

"Jack, people might not tell you so often how courageous you are. They might completely refuse to admit it, in fact. But they know it. Perhaps you were reckless, but someone had to step up and be reckless." Kate heard her own voice catch. She lowered her voice to a whisper and said the rest like a prayer. "Jack, I really need you to be okay. I could use your help, but also . . . I just really need you to be okay." She had instinctively bowed her head. When she glanced up, her eyes met Jack's. She found them absolutely alert. Twinkling.

He brought up his arms and clasped his hands behind his head. "It's always lovely to be needed. Anything else you have to say? I'm certainly coming around some, but maybe my brain is still foggy."

She smacked him. "Jack Haricot, honestly. Sometimes I really can't believe you." She paused. "How do you feel, though?"

"I feel like a courageous expert who has too often been underappreciated by my neighbors."

Kate rolled her eyes. "Are you thirsty? Because I'd be happy to go fetch you some water from that fetid river."

"Aw . . . don't be like that, Katie. You can sail in the winds of my bravery anytime."

She stood then and leaned back down toward him. She looked deeply into Jack's eyes, reached her arms around his neck, and released the belt with a snap. Jack thudded down into the dust.

"Seriously?" he said. "I don't see why you have to be like that."

"We should get moving. We must be getting close."

"Yeah? Is your evil detector sounding its alarm?"

"No, I think it's perfectly normal that a river runs green and smells rotten and has the ability to render a senseless boy even more senseless."

Jack stood up and heaved the pot of water over to a tall tree stump. One by one, he led each horse over to drink. Kate pretended not to notice how easy and logical he made caring for the creatures look. "Hey, Katie—"

"What?" she asked, but she refused to face him.

"I don't think you've acted too big for your britches. At all. I think you've surprised yourself lately and maybe even surprised me. You are pretty courageous, you know. All on your own."

Kate did not want to cry. But between her relief at Jack's improved health, her weariness at the long hours of hiking since they snuck off, and her fear of what terrible battle might lie in store, she couldn't help it. The tears eased out from the corners of her eyes.

Jack did not laugh at this. He did not ignore it, either.

"Aw, Katie. It's going to be all right. Thanks for taking care of me." Jack loaded the packs on the horses and boosted her up onto Lucius. "Even if taking care of me meant tying me to a horse with my own belt."

Kate and Jack laughed then. And then they set out, moving forward to face whatever it was that waited for them.

CHAPTER 12

"We need to follow along the trail of the river, without actually getting too close to the river." The authority had returned to Kate's voice. She paused to see if Jack would mock her.

But ahead of her, he merely nodded and called back, "You think it's related?"

"It has to be. That sulfuric smell signals evil presence." Kate wrinkled her nose, remembering it. "Unless there's another presence to contend with. But let's not even consider that, all right?"

"The fumes didn't affect you, though, did they?"

Kate had been waiting for him to bring that up. "Not as strongly as they affected you, but then again, I didn't move so close to the water."

"Yeah? It seemed like you were right there with me."

"Hmmmm." Kate made a noncommittal noise. "How do you think the horses are doing?"

"Kate." Jack slowed down so that they rode beside each other. "Do you think maybe your heritage has something to do with it? Maybe something in your blood makes you resistant?"

"You mean my Uncommon blood," Kate said flatly.

"Yeah. I do mean that." Jack leaned back in his saddle. "What are going to do—spend the rest of your life ashamed? You heard Sterling. There's nothing evil about it. You have extraordinary abilities—a set of weird talents. And we need to acknowledge them. As a team, we can use them to our advantage."

Kate regarded him carefully. After all, she'd really known Jack for only three days. But she'd never heard him say an insincere word. Kate believed she could trust him. "Honestly, I just don't know enough. Nan and I always avoided talking about it. I knew she was different. I feared I was. There was never anyone else I could ask. Mostly, in the village, people talked about me, and not to me."

Jack nodded. He knew all about that. Kate steeled herself and kept confiding. "Sometimes, I get these floods of feelings—like fear will just wash over me. It will immobilize me for a moment. I'll talk myself back up to the surface, saying, 'There's nothing to fear, Kate. You're imagining things.' Only to see something terrible happen hours or days later. So as I grew, it became hard to calm myself. Because I learned the pattern. Those feelings meant something awful waited on the horizon." Kate stopped talking, staring down at Lucius's sleek coat and waiting for Jack's judgment.

"That's it, though?" Jack asked casually.

Kate considered mentioning her recent strange and vivid dreams, but those were tricks that stress and worry had played on her. She wouldn't let Jack share that burden, too. So she shrugged and asked, "That's not freakish enough?"

"Not really. That just sounds like really keen instincts. The way the king and the constable spoke about you and your family, I'd hoped you could issue flames from your fingers or something. Levitate."

"Well, I'm so sorry for disappointing you, Jack." Sarcasm laced her voice, but in fact, Kate was a bit sorry. She'd witnessed Jack demonstrate all kinds of magic—the intricate hideaways he'd built, the way he'd moved calmly through the wolf pack as if he'd been raised among them. She wished she had more to contribute.

"I expect you just need training." He spoke matter-of-factly, as if there might be a school to attend—some kind of academy for the Uncommon. As if developing any magical gifts at all wouldn't earn her complete and immediate banishment from the village. "I hope you'll listen within yourself more. You know, if it comes down to fighting, or whatever we end up having to do for the sake of freeing Nan and Ella, you need to follow your gut and stop questioning yourself. Like watering the horses, for instance—filling the cooking pot wasn't such a lousy idea. Pretty sensible, actually."

"My shoes are still soaking wet, Jack," Kate argued mildly.

"Well, that's on account of our uncivilized horses. How rude of them to slurp!" He laughed then. "Katie, just trust yourself. That's all I'm saying. Trust yourself like you trust me."

The pair of them then rode comfortably enough, keeping the line of young trees by the waterline in sight and combing the ground ahead of them for any signs of something damaging in the area. Kate felt goofy about it, but she appreciated how Jack had worded it—*listening within herself.* As she rode, she tried to quiet all her mind's chatter so she could receive instruction from whatever force could help her. The more she listened for a message, though, the more she worried she might inadvertently invent one. Kate found self-confidence frustrating.

For most of her young life, she'd listened for the voice of Nan in her mind. She could jog loose a memory of her grandmother when she yearned for one or needed a valuable nugget of her wisdom. *A friend to all is a friend to none*, she might hear Nan say when she wondered for the thousandth time why Millicent Edwards stood as the most popular girl in the village even as she surely counted as the meanest. *Waste not, want not,* Nan's voice would offer when Kate stared down another pan of cracked corn at the seamstress's house.

She understood that she wasn't actually hearing Nan in those moments. She could conjure a memory of Nan when she needed to. That's how Kate, who lived alone for so much of her life, understood love. Small snippets of caring guidance: *Beauty in gloom is still beauty.* Or another of Nan's favorites: *Kindness is in our power, even when fondness is not.* Now, however, Kate strained to listen for Nan's voice. It pained her to hear only sayings her grandmother might have repeated hundreds of times over the years, when what she most hoped for was insight to help with today's frightful predicament. Beauty and kindness matter in every scenario is, of course, what Kate knew Nan would contend.

"I wish there was a way to warn Sterling about the water." It had been preying on her mind since she and Jack had regrouped and headed north again—the callousness of sneaking off and leaving the constable in the dark woods alone.

"No comment."

"It saved us each to journey with the other."

"Well, it saved me. We've established that."

"Yes, but it affected you first. And so I noticed. Otherwise, maybe I'd have just plowed on through and succumbed without warning. Sterling has no one."

"No comment," Jack repeated. But he couldn't help himself. "Except to say that Sterling probably knows all about the river," he muttered. "He probably helped dam it up." The silence that settled over them felt heavy and aggrieved. Jack sighed. "How about we stop talking about Sterling for a bit?" She shrugged, so he tried again. "Who do you think we're looking for? Who do you think is our true enemy?"

"I don't know of anyone so evil, Jack. Not beyond the ordinary kind of evil."

"No. I don't mean name them. Let's try to describe them. Who or what could actually build a castle like that and outfit those rooms so wickedly?"

"A witch. Right?"

"Yeah. That's my best guess. But a really powerful witch. Like leaves-Queen-Cecilia-quaking-in-her-boots kind of powerful. What would that kind of witch want with Nan?"

"I've been thinking about that," Kate spoke excitedly. "Remember what Sterling said?" Jack only groaned to hear the name brought up again. "No, seriously, remember what he said about the Uncommon? How society pushes them away, and their loneliness eventually compounds their situation?" Jack nodded.

"Well, Nan lived alone in that cottage in the woods for ages. Even my presence didn't change any of that. As soon as I was old enough to fend for myself, she sent me from one home to the next." Jack nodded again. He knew all that. Kate didn't intend to sound so pitiful. She was trying to explain the math. "So imagine how powerful her abilities must have gotten. Decades of being alone, at least five miles from the closest neighbor."

Jack reminded her of his own theory. "And all of that power would have made some witch insanely jealous."

"Maybe. Or maybe that evil presence decided to try to tap into some of Nan's powers. What if there's a way to do that?"

"Why keep those other prisoners? Ella and the other children in the tapestries? What could a witch or a demon or whatever gain from hurting them? And why direct those threats to you?"

That stumped her. They rode on in silence for a mile or two. Kate did not have to unpack the tapestries to remember the details. The dreadful scenes were seared into her mind. The utter hopelessness in the eyes of the girl with the razor in her hand. The grim panic of the children caught in that one room that had been bricked and baking like an oven.

As they rode, Kate kept thinking, but her eyes also skimmed the vegetation around the path, searching for the vine that Sterling had pointed out the night before. She wanted to find it, but she didn't want to find it. She urgently wanted to get to Nan, but she dreaded seeing her victimized. Kate felt determined and resolved—a soldier perched on her grand steed. But she also felt frightened—a coward half hoping she could simply ride on her fine horse along this path forever.

Every so often, a shadow fell over them and Kate had that feeling again of being watched from above. It made the skin on the back of her neck prickle. She shivered, grasping the saddle with both hands to steady herself. She shut her eyes so that the dizziness would not overcome her and tumble her from her mount.

When she opened her eyes, she found herself perched on a stool instead of a horse. The tingling on her neck had become an all-out cold. She felt different—lighter, more vulnerable. She tried to shake herself out of it and realized that she missed the weight of her hair, and the sensation of her curls bouncing around her shoulders. She reached up and found nothing. Her hands flailed, searching. They reached the velvety surface of her scalp—it felt like a chick, downy soft, newly hatched.

As her fingers traced her head, she found several angry cuts. Some had already scabbed over, some stung and oozed. She hadn't ever thought of herself as a vain person. But she felt tears burning the corners of her eyes, pooling in her throat as she choked back cries. Her whole head had been shorn. She felt freakish and ugly. She felt exposed.

She tried to calm herself by studying her surroundings. Another room—this one round, with a high, peaked ceiling and a single, forlorn window. She stood shakily and crept over to the window. The ground below seemed very far off. She had to squint to see a pair of benches below, blanketed with vines.

Directly behind her, she found an iron door. And beside that, a mirror. She forced herself to look.

She gasped. They weren't her eyes gazing back from her own reflection. Nor was it the shape of her head. Nor her bare neck. She opened her mouth to see someone else's lips drop open.

Still, there was no mistaking the grief shining in those eyes—even if they were blue and not green. Even if they were hers and not her own. She heard the cackle with the other girl's ears. It drifted from behind the iron door. "My goodness! Have three whole days passed already? Someone must need a haircut!"

She felt her knees buckle and searched desperately for an exit that didn't exist. She fell back onto the stool and sat there, resigned. When she heard the door open and the clicking heels announce their entrance into the room, Kate willed herself to stare straight ahead. She would not sacrifice a shred of the poor girl's dignity. She would not allow her captor to glimpse her own soul occupying the prisoner's eyes.

Instead, she focused on a tiny patch of blue sky framed by the window. As she felt the bony hands snap back her neck and the scrape of the straight razor against her scalp, she stared out into the blue. That's when she felt herself rising, rising . . .

When she felt settled again, she opened her eyes. Kate recognized the supple leather of the saddle, the powerful flanks of her trusted horse. She breathed deeply, reminding herself that she could not be swept away by strange dreams. Lucius had kept moving forward as always. She patted him, grateful for his steady, sure gait. Kate hoped Jack hadn't noticed her momentary drift. She looked up and scanned the trees for birds.

"Jack." She tried to hide the alarm in her voice. "Have you seen a bird lately? Any kind of bird?" Kate had feigned calm, but she hadn't tricked Lucius. He fretted, kicking up and snaking back and forth with nervousness. She patted the horse and cooed in his ear. Surely, Jack had seen some. She just hadn't been paying attention. "Jack?" she asked again.

"I haven't. And not a single critter, either. I haven't even seen a squirrel."

A coldness hit Kate's blood. She might have overlooked the small creatures that make their homes in the woods. But Jack wouldn't. Jack had been living among them for more than eighteen months, after all.

"We must be getting close," she murmured. She had hoped the journey would give her time to build up her reserves of bravery, but instead, the cold place in her belly simply spread. She thought she felt herself shivering and willed her body to remain still. That's when she realized it was her horse trembling. Lucius, too, felt fearful, but he kept forging ahead. Kate patted him lovingly, grateful for the lesson in courage her horse provided. "Attaboy, Lucius," she whispered.

Around them, the woods were gravely silent. No birdsong, no occasional snapping twig that indicated an animal in the vicinity. "How's it going, Jack?" she asked. She meant: *Is your heart pounding? Are your palms sweating so that it's hard to grip the reins?*

Jack understood. "I don't know. I feel like this is the worst stroll through the woods ever. It does make me appreciate having to climb that vine to kill the giant. At least then, there was something to distract me—finding a foothold, hoisting myself up. This feels like riding in doom." His voice dipped into a quieter place. "Katie, I'm a bit afraid, truth be told."

"I know. Me too. More than a bit." She would have thought that hearing Jack Haricot admit fear would inspire terror in her own heart. In fact, it had the opposite effect. She felt tougher somehow. Calmer. Nowhere near fearless, but more comfortable. She could breathe now. As she relaxed some, she felt Lucius's tremors ease.

We're all linked, Kate thought. *This is how we're all connected.*

The peace she felt had yet to descend on Jack. "Imagine the kind of malevolence able to empty the forest of animals," he said, his voice hitching in slow-building panic. "Just try to envision that, would you, please?" His horse reared slightly and Jack fought to keep him steady along the trail.

"Animals operate on instinct, too," Kate offered. "They might just be keeping a wary distance. You know, like after a forest fire."

"Sure, a forest fire. That's no big deal. An enemy as destructive as a forest fire. Maybe it's a dragon. That would cover all our bases, right?"

"It's not a dragon."

"You're sure now? You sound very certain."

"I am trusting myself. Just as you instructed."

"Wonderful. So no dragon. What. A. Relief."

Kate aimed to radiate strength and serenity. She imagined unfurling tranquil tendrils silently, stealthily—the way a spider drapes its web. She envisioned cloaking Jack with a sense of security and warmth—how it would settle over him like a flannel blanket on a cool night. Kate concentrated fiercely. She stared at him so intently that she believed her own thoughts had physically spun him around in the saddle. Because suddenly, Jack turned to her to speak. His face had broken into a wide smile.

"Good news, Kate. It's small, but at least it's something. A fly just buzzed right by my face!" He sounded so delighted, Kate considered just nodding and smiling. But she couldn't lie to Jack.

She tried to speak evenly, to line her voice in that soothing flannel. "Well, here's the thing. That's actually not a very positive sign, Jack. Traditionally, flies also indicate an evil presence."

"Is that so?" Jack couldn't hide his deflation. "How do you know that, Kate?" he challenged. "What makes you so sure?"

So she had to tell him. It was their role in nature.

"Flies feed off the dead."

CHAPTER 13

They rode another fifty feet before the swarm hit them.

Kate saw it first and swore to herself that it looked like smoke billowing in a small clearing in the trees. The sound it made didn't seem natural. At the village distillery, old Evans had built a contraption that used pouring water to turn a set of gears, which then spun an enormous cylinder, which in turn shook barley through a wire sieve. The sound of the cloud ahead of them was like that—clumsy and mechanical. Oversize and determined.

Jack's horse startled and bucked. Kate watched him tear his sleeve from his shirt and try to cover the horse's face. She understood that the cloud had blinded the animal and that had spooked him. Kate looked down, searching for fabric for Lucius. She'd stashed her apron in her dress pocket when she woke up that morning at Jack's. She remembered feeling self-conscious about dressing as a servant. That seemed like years before.

The apron worked well. The horse could see through its light muslin fabric, and Kate was able to fasten the strings firmly. Lucius didn't even break stride. To protect herself from the flies, Kate used her horse's mane. She buried her face in the long, jet-black strands and held tight to the reins. She clamped her mouth shut and held her nose as long as she could.

The flies still crept in. In front of her, Jack looked outlined by a blur. She heard him sputtering and choking and noticed that his horse kept veering toward the river. Kate understood the instinct. The water offered relief from the insects. Of course, the horse couldn't understand that the river offered poison as well.

"Jack!" she shouted, even though it cost her as her mouth filled with flies. Kate hacked and spat. "Stay away from the river, Jack!" The buzzing overwhelmed her ears. She could not tell if he heard her. She felt the thousands of tiny wings beating against her skin and fought the urge to vomit.

She needed to scream. Her fear and frustration boiled up—she could not hold those emotions in any longer. But the swarm still thrummed around her. Her whole body vibrated with it. She knew if she cried out, the flies would dive for her open mouth.

She would not surrender like that. She would not allow herself to be smothered by the light wings of insects.

Instead, she imagined her terror and rage as a silvery ball in the pit of her gut. She pictured it growing, the way a snowball grows when you roll it in more snow. She envisioned rolling the ball of terror up to her throat. Instead of spitting it out in an explosion of sound, she guided it away from her mouth and saw it travel up to her brain. Once there, she finally allowed herself to unleash the emotion. She imagined hurling that ball, how it would explode into tiny particles of light. Kate could see that happen. She could hear her scream echo in her mind. Her whole head filled with the noise, in a satisfying crescendo. For a moment, it felt freeing. Kate knew she'd never yell that loudly in real life.

Amazingly, she felt better. Just imagining her feelings vocalized brought relief. And even more amazingly, the cloud of flies lifted. They left her skin. She watched the swarm rise above her and Lucius. It connected with the cloud floating up from Jack. Gradually, the horrible sound of them faded. She heard a buzz instead, and as the swarm rose up in the sky, even the buzz dissipated into silence.

"Holy saints, Kate. Remind me to never throw you a surprise party," Jack quipped, but his voice shook. She also heard the hoarseness in his throat from all the choking. He must have hopped down to guide the horse away from the river. His face was streaked in dust and smeared bugs, his hair disheveled. But he was fine, joking with her and comforting the nervous horse.

"You heard me?" she asked excitedly. "You could hear me scream?"

"It seems the whole forest heard you scream. That's when the bug fog lifted."

"I didn't open my mouth," she told him. He narrowed his eyes, dubious. "Really, Jack. I couldn't. The flies were all around me. I would have drowned in them."

"So I heard you . . ."

"In your head! I pictured my voice as a great ball of emotion and made it burst in my mind instead of springing from my mouth." As Kate described it, she realized it didn't sound quite so magical out loud. It sounded weird.

But Jack understood. "That's fantastic." He helped her check Lucius for injuries, telling her, "The flies buzzing threw me off. They'd coated me." He shuddered, remembering. "But then this scream rang out. Kate—let me just say that you've got a set of clairvoyant lungs on you. If there'd been any imaginary glass nearby, you would have shattered it. You sounded so close to me, as if you'd shouted in my ear. It almost made me angry. But then I saw how far back you actually were and so the sound I heard didn't quite make sense." He glanced up. "It makes sense now. Do you think it was the picturing it? More than the wanting it?"

Kate considered that. "I think visualizing it helped. But I think it happened because I wanted so desperately to call out a warning." And then because that embarrassed her and because the next was also true, she added, "Also I've been only pretending to stay calm, so all those pent-up feelings needed to burst forth."

"Oh, but you're such a good pretender," Jack teased. "Thank you for warning me. I don't like bugs. You'd think after living in a hole in the ground for a year, we'd have called a truce by now, but I don't care for the creepy crawlies at all."

Kate brushed some dead flies from Lucius's eyes as Jack searched through the food pack for a reward for their loyal steeds. He found carrots, and both horses warily munched, perhaps a bit tired of the strange, warped biology they'd confronted in their journey thus far.

"So we know you can send unspoken messages under extreme circumstances. Let's set the goal of sending them more casually next. I'll do my best to tune in. Perhaps that means quieting my mind? You ought to know that will take a real effort—my mind is often so active with deep thoughts and philosophical ruminations." Jack smiled wryly. "So just keep trying."

"I shall try to cut through your philosophy whenever possible," Kate replied. "Meanwhile, I wonder if we should walk the horses now."

"What would be the benefit?"

"Safety. It might give us more control if we run into trouble again."

"Safety for whom, though? We're better protected from most predators on horseback."

"But, Jack, the horses—they don't know how to fight those enemies." Kate brushed her fingers through Lucius's mane, trying to untangle the knots she'd put there while hiding her face.

"Kate, they're not pets. And horses aren't supposed to fight enemies. We are. Doing so on horseback gives us an advantage." She stared at him reproachfully. "Listen—soldiers ride horses. That's the way."

"But soldiers expect to fight a certain adversary. We don't know who or what we'll face. It seems needlessly cruel to subject the horses to that. When it came down to it, if you hadn't been able to regain control, you would have had to let your horse run for the water."

Jack didn't even need time to consider. "Yes. That's true."

"The horse would have died."

"Also true."

"And you would have forgiven yourself?"

"Forgiven myself? I would never have blamed myself. It would have been sad to lose the horse, to know that he suffered. But it would have been on account of those damn flies. I did my best to care for the horse."

He had, Kate knew. She recalled how he had torn his sleeve. His first thought had been for the horse.

Jack continued. "But let me be clear—I cared for the horse because I needed him. Had he panicked and thrown me, I would have succumbed. We're using these horses, just as we'll use the weapons the king provided."

"I see it differently." Kate would not budge. "If we lead these horses into a certain horrific death, that qualifies as cruelty. The prospect of it will distract me from our mission. I'll lose the ability to concentrate and that will sacrifice our advantages."

"This is a foolish argument to pick, Kate."

"I'm not arguing. We disagree on this one issue."

Jack sighed. "Very well. We ride the horses until we both decide we've come too close to danger. Then we leave them with food and water and hope to return to them. That, too, may count as cruel, though. These are magnificent horses. They've been trained for battle."

Kate mounted Lucius. "It's not their battle. But I accept your compromise." She picked up the reins. "Shall we forge ahead, then?"

"Sure." Jack threw up his hands in defeat. He gathered the rest of the supplies and swung himself up to ride. "It's great to know you've developed this deep emotional bond with the horses.

I suppose you'll next tell me you've begun communicating clairvoyantly with the beasts."

"You don't even know your horse's name."

"Remember when you thought I'd been struck dumbfounded forever? How kindly you treated me then? Let's try that out again, please."

"I'm sorry, Jack." Kate spoke sheepishly. "I do feel like I've forged a connection with the animals, though. They mustn't feel discarded at the end of this. That's all."

He exhaled and lightly rubbed his own horse's flank. "It's all right. We'll make sure to return them to their luxurious stalls on King Wilhelm's grounds. Long after this venture hits the storyteller's book, these horses will be better fed and better rested than you and me."

"Well, I will try to reassure them of that by speaking clairvoyantly," Kate kidded. The lighthearted talk helped smooth the tension between her and Jack, and it also jogged loose a thought that had been caught in the back of her mind. "Do you think the horses heard me scream? You know, in their heads."

Jack considered. "Maybe. Hard to tell if they were shook up because of the bugs or if you were the one who really scared them. I know one thing, though: The flies heard. As soon as your scream rang out in my head, those flies immediately lifted."

"That's right." Kate had been so caught up in the swarm's aftermath that she hadn't considered the ramifications. "So that probably means others heard."

"Like Sterling."

Kate chose to ignore the sneer in Jack's voice. "Maybe Nan," she suggested. "And whoever took her. That person might have heard me, too."

She hoped it might have scared the captor.

But more likely, it had given warning.

They'd find out soon enough.

CHAPTER 14

Jack spotted the first vine almost accidentally. He'd been searching for some birch bark to make a salve for his shoulder. He'd admitted to Kate that his joints throbbed after his last struggle with the horse and he worried about holding up a crossbow. Birch salve was a quick fix. So when they crested another hill and Jack saw a line of white trees, he whistled to let Kate know he needed to stop.

The vine wove in and out of the slender trunks of birch, and Kate figured Jack was focused on finding the loosest patch of bark possible. That meant the rains might have had the chance to creep in and that moistness would make the minerals inside the bark easier to scrape. "This stuff is magical!" Jack called out. "I swear by it. You should seriously try some."

"I'm not sore any longer." Kate wasn't. Her body had adjusted to the horse's jostling and was handling the journey better than she would have expected. She felt like a warrior. Besides, having spent years denying an involvement in witchcraft, Kate shied away from home remedies.

Jack crouched down, scraping out the bark's lining with his knife and pounding it between two flat rocks.

"Where did you learn to make this?" Kate asked him, mostly just making conversation, waiting to get moving again.

"My mom," Jack answered. "Her pains became quite unbearable toward the end. She taught me how to make this medicine, and it did seem to ease the aching a bit."

Kate swallowed the lump in her throat. "I'm sorry, Jack."

He looked up, surprised. "No, it's a good memory. I hated seeing my mother so ill, but I had the chance to tend to her. And that way, she taught me salves and remedies. Living alone, it's proven quite useful. And later, when I have my own family to care for, it will still come in handy."

He finished pounding and quickly unbuttoned his shirt. Kate averted her eyes and carefully memorized the intricate leatherwork on her saddle. Her mind's ability to stray to the shallow subject of romance during even the most solemn of moments continued to vex her. Thankfully, Jack didn't seem to notice. He cupped the pulp in his hand and rubbed it into his chiseled shoulder. Kate forced herself to think about the fetid river, the flies, even the tapestries rolled up in her pack.

Jack sighed heavily. "So much better. You're sure I can't rub some on your shoulders, Kate?"

She almost gasped. "I'm positive! Thank you, though." She hoped she wasn't accidentally radiating her thoughts into his mind. She grumbled to herself, "For heaven's sake, Kate, get ahold of yourself. It's like you're possessed."

"What's that?" Jack asked.

"Nothing. I was just reminding myself of some kind of song I used to sing as a girl." She trailed off, mortified, half hoping the evil they searched for would open up the earth so she could fall through to its fiery core.

"No, I mean, what's that?" Jack buttoned his shirt with one hand and pointed at the base of the birch tree with the other. "They're leaves the shape of spades, Kate! Dark green and shot through with gold veins." Kate's embarrassment evaporated. She hopped from the saddle and approached the plant carefully, as if she thought the vine might attack her.

She picked up a thin branch and poked at the vine. "Did you touch it?"

"I don't know." Jack sounded flustered. "Should I not have?"

"It just looks like a plant."

"But it's *the* plant."

"I think it is."

"Do you think it's poisonous?"

"Do you feel poisoned?"

Jack glared at her in response.

"I doubt it's poisonous," she assured him. "Really. You look perfectly well. And besides, in the tapestries, the plant was growing inside some of the cells."

"Right," Jack said impatiently. He rubbed his arms, as if checking for bruising or numbness. "Why is that a good thing, again?"

"Well, those prison cells basically function as torture chambers. It wouldn't make sense for someone to leave a poisonous plant accessible. That would be an act of mercy, right? That doesn't fit our profile."

Kate's logic seemed to placate Jack. He crouched down to get a closer look. "It has to be it. I've never run across it in my part of the woods. But it doesn't look ominous, does it?"

Kate used the branch in her hand to lift the vine. When she did so, she saw that the plant wound around each tree. It seemed to continue up the hill—she couldn't see where it ended. "Well, do we just follow it?"

"Because trailing vegetation worked out so well for me last time?"

Kate stood up and gathered a few more sticks. She tucked them into her pack and pulled the pack down from Lucius. "We decided, right? We go on foot now."

At first, she thought he'd refuse to answer. Jack stood gazing up the hill. She could see him chewing on the inside of his lip. Finally, he nodded slowly.

"Yep. We did agree on that." He walked over to the pair of trusty horses. "We'll leave the pot full of water. Doubt we'll be cooking anyway. Leave the saddles on. That should keep them calm and remind them that we'll come back for them. We'll tie them to those trees over there."

"Are you sure about tying them?" Kate swallowed hard and forced herself to ask the practical question. "What if we don't come back? I mean—"

"I know what you mean, Katie. We'll come back." Jack chucked her lightly on her shoulder.

"Right, but seriously, what if we don't? I don't want them to be tied here, left to starve. Or worse. We don't know what kind of wild animals roam around at night."

She patted Lucius's muzzle and tried to send him a silent message of thanks and love.

"We won't tie them tightly. If something spooks them enough to kick up, they'll break loose easily."

Kate searched Jack's face for any inkling of deceit. He noticed.

"I promise, Kate. That's what people do. The reins will reassure the horses. But if they need to race out of here—well, they're powerful animals. We're leaving thoroughbreds, not old mares." He grabbed his pack and gave his dark-brown horse an offhand pat on the flank. "I'm not going to start lying to you over horses."

She nodded and gulped. She knew that. She understood that she was just stalling. As much as she didn't want to endanger the horses, she didn't want to leave them, either. It meant halving their tiny brigade.

She allowed herself one last embrace of Lucius's neck and even patted Jack's horse for good measure. Then she started forward, without looking back or waiting for Jack to catch up.

"We're really just going to follow the plant?" he asked her.

"Do you have a better idea?"

Jack's silence served as an answer.

Every once in a while, they ran out of vine. The plant seemed to stop abruptly and then Kate would back up and poke under the last piece with a stick. They'd see how it continued upward. Sometimes it snaked under moss or dead leaves. Sometimes rocks covered it. Without fail, though, Jack and Kate could dig around until the next segment of vine rose up to lead them.

That certainty set off alarm bells in Jack's mind. "Have you even seen a plant stretch so far?" he asked Kate. "I mean one plant that stretched for miles? Up a mountain?"

"What are you thinking?"

"I'm thinking that we're following this one clue very closely. I'm worried that with our eyes on the dirt, we might be missing something else. It feels too convenient—like something's leading us in one particular direction, up an extremely specific path."

"Let's slow down, then. Try to be more aware of our surroundings."

"Okay. But I want to check something first." Jack stopped and rummaged in his pack. He pulled out Nan's pillowcase.

"Jack, we know it's the vine in the tapestries." Really, Kate didn't want to see the needlework again. She fought to keep herself focused and brave, but reviewing the devastating weavings threatened to unravel her resolve. They'd confront the actual castle soon enough. She didn't want to see any more pictures of it.

"Just wait for a minute, will you?" Jack implored. "I need to see something again."

Kate heard him suck in his breath sharply.

"What is it?" she asked. "What did you need to see?"

"Maybe you should wait with the animals."

"What? What did you just say to me?" Kate reared her head like a spooked horse.

"I'm serious. You can do your emotional visualization thing and listen for me to send a mind message if I need help." And then, because that suggestion sounded hollow and ridiculous, Jack added, "Most likely, I won't need help, though. I'm better off going solo, you know? That's how I took out the giant. I really think that's our best bet."

"I think you should just tell me what's going on." Kate held out her open palm. "Let me see the tapestry."

Jack rolled it up carefully. He seemed to take forever.

"Jack," she ordered. "Give it here, please."

It was the tapestry they'd found with Ella's horse. It showed the princess sitting in a pile of ash, chained to a wall. Her reddened hands looked as painful as they had the first time Kate had viewed the scene. "What is it, Jack? We're supposed to be a team, right? What are you seeing that I'm still missing?"

He looked miserable. "We zeroed in on the illustration, Kate. Of course we did—it's petrifying. But maybe that was the point. The picture served as a distraction." He brought out another scroll, the last one they'd found at Nan's cottage, with its angry, embroidered scrawl. "Don't you see? *It should have been you.* And then *You're next.* Someone directed those messages to you, Kate. Your grandmother, Ella, even those other missing children—what if they're all just bait? What if someone has gone to all this trouble to create a trap for you? That vine is leading you right into it." Jack buried his head in his hands. "And I spotted it. I pointed out the stupid plant to you. I helped set you up."

Kate didn't think what Jack was saying made any sense. Why would anyone want *her*?

And yet . . . it made some sense, too. She couldn't explain why. But it did.

Jack pressed on. "Let me go on my own. Whoever it is—they won't expect that. After all, I'm the selfish brat who almost brought down all of Shepherd's Grove for a bit of silver. You've brought me this far."

"That's a lovely gesture, Jack." Kate wasn't being sarcastic. Aside from her grandmother taking her in, it was just about the kindest thing anyone had ever offered her. "But you know I can't agree to that." She traced the letters of the messages with her finger. "I read these. They just didn't really sink in. Or maybe they did and I just refused to acknowledge them. Maybe this whole time, they idled in the back of my mind and I just needed to reach a place where I could accept them. Because if I'm wanted as an adversary, then I'll show up as an adversary. You knew the giant was your fight and so you took him on alone. Maybe this is my battle." She grinned up at him. "That would mean *you* should stay back with the horses."

Jack set his jaw. "That's not about to happen."

"Okay, then. Don't ask me to turn back."

Jack refused to meet her eyes. At first, she worried that he'd continue to debate her. She'd made a sound argument, though. It was the only path to take, and she understood enough about Jack's sense of honor to know that he'd see it that way, too.

"Katie Hood. You showed up like some drowned rat at my doorstep. You couldn't even land on the ground properly. I expected I'd have to carry you through the woods on my back."

Kate smiled ruefully. "I'm happy to have surprised you."

"Oh, you've surprised me, for certain. You are quite an amazing woman." He exhaled slowly. "So we'll keep going together. But from now on, we handle the approach differently. Just because the bait's been set, we don't have to spring the trap." He reached over, took the stick from her, and began drawing a diagram on the muddy forest floor.

"I'll keep tracking the ivy. And I'll make myself relatively obvious. Someone will be checking, I'm sure of it. While I trail the plant, you'll hike parallel to me, but several feet off to the side. When we get in view of the castle or prison or whatever, you'll widen the distance and pick up your pace. That way, you'll approach from the flank. It'll give you a wider view of the action, and maybe, if we play it absolutely correctly, a chance at a surprise attack. Sound good?" He waited patiently and let her study it carefully.

“It’s pretty solid, as far as plans go,” Kate announced. “But it leaves you out there as a sitting duck. Don’t think you can sacrifice yourself without me noticing.”

“It’s not a sacrifice. It won’t kill me.” Jack spoke with absolute certainty. “If I get captured, I’ll become more bait—something else used to draw you out into the open.”

Kate almost reminded him of the cells in the tapestries, how he might prefer a quick execution to whatever creative torture was invented to elicit his suffering. But Jack had seen the same illustrations she had. She wouldn’t belittle him by implying that he did not know all that he risked.

“Let’s do it,” she said.

And so Kate and Jack both stood, smiled slightly at each other, and split their paths.

CHAPTER 15

Kate did not let herself linger near Jack before heading away from him. There was no point, she knew. Nothing else to say. She kept a careful eye on him as he hiked, occasionally bending over to uncover another segment of vine before continuing on. Jack was too smart to look over at her. That would blow her cover and defeat the entire purpose of splitting up. She knew he understood this, had probably realized it before she had. Still, Kate felt lonely scurrying along beside him, unseen.

She focused on him, taking note every time he stopped or slowed. Kate had never felt so important in her entire life. The idea that someone had built a prison, full of rooms devoted to torment, just to lure her out of her inconsequential daily existence seemed completely insane. *So I'm dealing with someone mad*, she thought. *In a short while, I'll be challenging some lunatic intent on destroying all I know and love.*

Every now and then, an odor hit her. Just like the smell emanating from the river, but possibly worse. It came in waves. At first, it almost overcame her. One minute, she was walking, crouched down and skulking through the tallest grasses she could find. The next, she felt herself swaying, sickened by the scent that she now associated with swarms of insects.

The thought of Jack kept her upright. She knew he'd be forging ahead, trusting her to keep his pace. If she collapsed, he might not realize it. He'd keep tracking, and eventually reach the castle. Most likely, he'd be captured or killed. If she let herself fall, sickened in the weeds, Jack would suffer for no reason at all. And no one—not him, not Nan—could ever count on rescue.

After a while, Kate understood the smell was in her mind. That didn't make it less real, but she stopped trying to cover her mouth and nose to escape it. Instead, she picked out a piece of greenery on her path. Some wild chives grew in a shady spot, some fresh pine. She would not allow her own imagination to defeat her, even as she felt the weight of her fear blanketing her like a wet swath of wool.

She checked her weapons frequently. It got so she had a routine, like a dance she repeated. She could almost count out the steps: dagger in her waistband, knife in her boot, bow slung across her back.

Kate wouldn't be able to strike first with her weapons, though. She expected that would be her instinct, and she told herself that she'd have to fight against the impulse. Say she ever lucked out enough to strike hard, fast, and first. She would have no guarantee of rescuing the victims. She'd need to ensure their freedom first.

Out of the blue, she found herself thinking about her parents. She knew there was danger in that. Even with all the years that had accumulated since, the loss of her mother and father filled her with the kind of raw grief that could sideline concentration. She could not afford to sink into sobs or childish *what-ifs*.

Kate knew that once upon a time, her parents had also decided on a hard path. They had polished their weapons and crammed packs with supplies, then headed out to an uncertain future. She had not been coddled. When they left, no one had pretended they would return. Now she wondered: Had her mother held the slimmest belief in her own survival? Kate had struggled to leave the horse she'd ridden for three days. How had her mother left behind her own child?

Kate ached for the girl she could have been. Because her parents' choice had marked her, too. She imagined the armor of mournfulness hardening around her. She visualized her parents' resolve fortifying her own intentions.

To her left, Jack's dark hair bobbed through the greenery like a bird taking flight and then settling. He had described the two of them as disposable orphans. But they'd become irreplaceable to each other. At least, she could not replace him.

Kate shook her head at her own foolishness. He was climbing a mountain, serving as decoy, and still she struggled to believe in his regard for her. Above her, the sky was an indisputable blue. For a moment, she allowed herself to feel the true intensity of her feelings for Jack. And then she let them float away in order to concentrate on fighting for both their lives.

Just then, Jack stood up with his hands on his hips—a signal they'd chosen in advance. She hurried through the thick vegetation, trying to draw near. Her calves stretched to increase her stride. A few yards ahead, she, too, halted. Not right beside him, still slightly behind.

Kate bit her lip, steeled herself, and looked up.

CHAPTER 16

It was more a fortress than a castle. Unlike King Wilhelm's grand estate, there were no signs of luxury attached to the grim building on the horizon. No velvet crested flags hung from the turrets. No windows gaped from the impenetrable facade. Had Kate just wandered through the forest and found it, she would have expected this castle to be abandoned. Except for the almost crippling nausea she felt, she would not have attributed evil to the place. Just an utter blankness. A void of hope or grief.

Now as she confronted it, she understood the barrenness to be its own kind of evil. She hunkered down, her eyes riveted to Jack, and waited for the enemy to make a move. It didn't take long, and it began with vultures. Several swooped down, pecking at Jack's head and neck. She curbed herself and did not interfere.

Initially, Jack didn't call out for her or for anyone else. He sank to his knees, screamed, and batted at the birds with his hands. She watched them jab at him, and she concentrated on sending him reassurance. Kate told herself that as long as she kept Jack in her sight, he could not fall. But the vultures collected above him, as if they already considered him a carcass. She could no longer see him through the throng of dark wings.

Kate's empathy kicked up. She experienced Jack's terror, how the greasy feathers beat against his face. She knew the birds echoed the earlier swarm of flies, but instead of the light movement along his body that had caused his skin to tingle and crawl, the vultures snapped at his skin with hooked beaks. They dug into his shoulders with powerful talons.

She felt Jack's pain and panic even before she saw him rise from the ground. Kate bit her fist to keep from screaming as she witnessed the birds carry him off. When he did call out a name, he bellowed, "Calista!" This was Jack's own sick version of a joke. He would not give up her presence in the grasses, but he might dare her to cause some kind of jealous scene. Just for fun. Just so they'd have something to laugh about after.

Kate darted toward the castle in quick bursts. Every so often, she forced herself to stop, take stock of her surroundings, and choose her next steps. Jack's abduction had been orchestrated to horrify. The birds might be too brainless to detect they had snatched the wrong orphan, but Kate knew it would take only seconds for the malevolent presence she faced to see Jack and redirect its rage.

So Kate ran from cover to cover, up the flank.

At first, she could track Jack in the sky. Then, in an abrupt squall of beating wings and bellows, she lost him. Here and there, scattered about the grass, were black feathers. Kate knew Jack had probably ripped them out, intending to leave a trail.

As she closed in, waves of sickness crashed over her. She tasted bile in her throat. Her eyes stung and watered. And then Kate heard a voice, clear and distinct.

"I know that you are there, waiting and watching. I can feel you, just as I feel the tips of my fingers at the end of my arm."

She could swear the voice was Nan's . . . except not. Same tone, same register, but the cadence was different. This voice spoke more slowly, more deliberately.

"Come forward, Katherine."

She knew then it was not Nan. Her grandmother never called her by her full name.

She also realized the voice had not spoken aloud. It had carried itself into her head. She heard it just as she felt her own pulse ticking faster.

"Come forward, Katherine. Before you force me to start hurting him."

Kate tried to listen past the beckoning. She combed through the silence for Jack's voice but detected nothing. *Jack.* She sent out tendrils, searching. The voice returned as a hiss.

"He cannot answer you right now. Keep listening, though, out there in the cover of trees. Soon enough, you'll hear him weeping."

Kate tried to shut down her senses. She visualized building a wall, stone by stone, to fence in her thoughts. That worked, somewhat; she could barely hear anything besides the deep quiet of the empty woods. Here and there, though, the eerie peels of laughter would seep in. She clenched her jaw and refused to let it provoke her.

She and Jack hadn't planned for this part. There hadn't been a way to map out storming a castle they couldn't even see. Kate steadied herself. She rooted within for her own instinct. And everything inside told her to run.

So Kate sprinted. She did not dash straight for the fortress. Instead, she crisscrossed through the birches and brambles, hoping to avoid detection as long as she could. Right at the last traverse, she wavered for the slightest second. Then she raced forward and threw herself against soaring iron doors.

She braced for an impact that never came. The doors eased open as she shouldered against them, causing her to stumble through. Kate had not pictured herself facing off in battle from a clumsy pile on the stone floor. Her body ached from the jolt and fall. As she fought to raise her head, she spotted a lone, black feather beside her. She sprang to her feet and drew her knife from her boot.

She'd tumbled into a hall not unlike the one in King Wilhelm's palace. This one looked positively cavernous in comparison, though. No guards, no shields, no flickering chandeliers. Just a long table, stretching over most of the room's length, bookended by two chairs. At the far end, a woman sat. Stunned, Kate lowered her stabbing hand. Her eyes flickered over another version of Nan.

"A rather uncivilized entrance." Kate recognized the voice as the one she'd tried to block. The one that sounded so much like her grandmother's. "I would have thought you'd been raised better than that." The woman also looked like Nan, had Nan been given the chance to lead a more comfortable life. Instead of the long strands of silver, this woman's hair was arranged in an elaborate braid. Over the years, Nan's eyes had seemed to disappear in creases; her mouth had sprung deep parentheses from laughing. This woman's face remained smooth and unworn. She wore a velvet dress, violet colored and gathered at the bodice. Below the waist, the fabric billowed out in a full skirt.

Kate registered another difference and immediately glanced away, as if polite discretion somehow counted in her current situation. One of the woman's arms looked normal, even lovely—without the loose skin and age spots that marked Nan's age. The other arm looked different. It hung shriveled from her right sleeve—shrunken and grotesque.

The woman smirked. "Oh, this? Don't feel bad. The body learns to adjust. It only occasionally interferes with physical tasks. Weaving, for instance—out of the question. But that's fine. Recently, I've acquired some help."

"Where is my Nan?" Kate felt grateful to be able to keep her voice steady.

"Occupied." The woman drummed the fingertips of her good hand on the scarred table. "I thought we could catch up. Get to know each other. You've been robbed, Katherine, of the chance to adore me. But I intend to right that wrong." Her voice carried on, lush and hypnotizing. "You've been robbed of a great deal. We have that in common. Perhaps we have that in Uncommon as well." She flashed the smirk again.

"I'm sure we don't," Kate declared. "I don't even know who you are."

"Well, that's easily remedied, dear. I'm your grandmother's sister, your great-aunt Caterina. It's for my sake you were named.

Do you understand what that means, Kate? Why, I'm the closest thing you've got to a fairy godmother!" This time the smirk broke into laughter—a cackle that exposed her as the witch she was.

Kate edged her way along the table. She tried to calculate whether it made more sense to lunge at the woman or to rush through the castle, freeing prisoners from cells. She had never slit anyone's throat before—not even a small animal's, for meat. She worried about the physical logistics. Caterina's white and slender neck looked easy enough to miss. What if her knife got lodged in the gore and gristle? How did one yank one's weapon out of a bleeding body?

And Kate knew enough about witches to expect that the cells she needed to spring open would not be unlocked with a ring of keys. They'd be enchanted. Maybe if she killed Caterina, those spells would break. That's how it went in the witch stories told at festival time. But could she gamble the lives of Jack and her Nan on folktales?

Kate felt frozen with indecision. Her hand tightened around the knife's grip. Caterina only looked bored.

Sit down, the witch commanded. Kate heard the command in her veins. *Move*, Kate told herself. But she stood rooted to the spot. "Sit *down*." The second time, Caterina spoke her directive aloud.

At least speak, Kate instructed herself. The same dizzying sickness that had seized her in the woods clenched her in its grip now. The pressure on her chest felt familiar in its awfulness. She clutched at her throat, fighting to breathe.

"The illness that you suffer from is called cowardice. It runs on your side of the family," Caterina sneered. "You would prefer to be poisoned. I know. That would provide a villain for you to blame. But I didn't cause you to drag your heels up that mountain. It took a bit of algae in the river and suddenly you've succumbed to grave disease."

Trickery. Kate would not allow herself to be manipulated. "The flies," she croaked.

"Flies are drawn to the unwashed. Perhaps they mistook you for a little pig." Caterina cackled again. The sound hurt Kate's teeth—like metal scraping against metal.

"If we're family, why didn't you just invite me here? Why the disappearances, the tapestries? Why all of this?" Kate kicked at the feather on the stone floor before her.

"In actuality, I don't much care for family." Caterina leaned forward in her seat. "Really, it's a simple transaction. My terms: You stay. Your grandmother stays. The others go free, including the royal ingénue and young Master Haricot." She clicked her tongue, as if the pairing had just then occurred to her. "Look how that works out! Perhaps she can console him?" She grimaced.

"Oh, but!" She held up her hands. "The young brother and sister pair are dead. That was by no means intentional—a misread temperature gauge. My apologies."

The witch didn't sound a bit sorry.

Kate imagined lunging. How the knife would meet resistance at first and then she'd need to twist it. She could do that and then search every corner of the castle, every hidden passage, every cold corridor. Jack would have fought to leave more feathers to guide her. She could take the time to focus and reach Nan through sheer will and belief. She could fight past all the remnants of malice left behind in the castle even if she managed to execute Caterina. She could free the other prisoners and help lead them back through the dense woods. She could continue to struggle.

For the first time since Kate had crested Birch Hill, the dull and almost imperceptible roar in her ears quieted. Finding the cottage abandoned, examining the tapestries, the mob of villagers. Even as Jack held a blade to her throat two nights before. Since she first saw the wolves gathered outside her grandmother's cottage, she'd been afraid and uncertain. Accepting Caterina's offer meant she would no longer need to feel uncertain. Kate understood there were things in the world that were fated. And she'd always known that membership in her family carried with it an odd destiny. Her parents had made a sacrifice almost a decade before. Perhaps it was her turn.

She tried to detach herself and consider her life honestly. Had it not been for the past few days, no one would miss her or Nan. She'd done a good deed—she had drawn Jack out of hiding. He would lead Ella to the clearing in the forest. He'd boost her up onto Lucius and ride beside her on the horse he refused to name. He'd return to Shepherd's Grove as a hero with a princess and fat purse. Jack was practical. He would come to see the benefit. And the other prisoners should never have been in cells to begin with. They'd been used as pawns, probably first to ensnare her grandmother and then herself in Caterina's web.

"You are Uncommon." Kate didn't even know why she said it. Why it mattered. She supposed she wanted to understand.

"Darling, I'm more than Uncommon. I am extraordinary."

"Born Nan's twin?" Kate asked. Caterina nodded languidly, slightly smiling. Her eyes sparkled. She appeared keen to hear Kate put the pieces together. "But with a noticeable difference." Kate gestured toward her arm. Caterina's gaze narrowed slightly, but she nodded slowly all the same.

"Was someone cruel about that?" Kate pried.

The witch lifted her chin in defiance. "I was only doted upon."

"All the same, it must have been difficult: To have a mirror image, but to be the warped reflection. Painful for a child." Kate let the last bit sink in. She hoped it hurt to remember. "You were both raised as Uncommon." Kate knew from Nan that back then, the education of the Uncommon entailed lessons held in secret. "You felt powerful," she told Caterina. "But Nan was just as powerful." Kate could see it as images unspooling in her head. The girls studying and practicing. Discovering their abilities together, just as Caterina was discovering her limitations, the way the world considered her the flawed version. Kate felt heavy with pity for the girl. She thought she might weep.

Caterina smiled and clasped her hands. "Ah, that's your empathy stirring—the greatest hindrance of the Uncommon. You feel it even for me."

"You found a way to quiet it in yourself."

"No. I silenced it."

"You welcomed evil."

"Yes. It made me mighty. More so than my simpleminded sister could ever understand. It got so I couldn't stand to look at her—"

"Because of her arms?"

"Because of her absolute lack of ambition." Caterina spat out the words. "So I left. Onward. Upward. I met a man. I had a daughter."

"You named her Cecilia."

"You're quicker than your grandmother . . . I'll give you that."

"Why do you need us?"

Caterina shrugged. "Everything is a transaction. You must offer the wickedness room in yourself. As it ages, it grows. So the older one gets, the more space it demands. I'd like to keep this form." She glanced down at herself. "It pleases me to have grown into a great beauty. So I need more bodies for the . . . overabundance of spirit."

"But why us in particular? Do you still hate Nan that much?"

Caterina kept licking her lips. She reminded Kate of a lizard, flicking her tongue around her cold-blooded mouth. "No. Well, yes. But that's beside the point. My particular guests are fond of my Uncommon blood."

So those stood as the specific terms. Kate wouldn't just doom herself to be locked in some dungeon, furnished with sick and complex tortures. She'd be overtaken. It would take years of feeling herself gradually draining away. She would sense the evil replacing her, cell by cell, until eventually she'd lose herself completely. And the whole time it happened, she would know that she had burdened Nan with the same fate.

Kate finally lowered herself into the chair at the opposite end of the long table. "I have my own demands," she said.

Caterina yelped with laughter. "That's adorable."

"I'll give you another way to shatter my grandmother." A perfectly sculpted eyebrow raised, interest piqued. "Keep us in separate cells." In the far recesses of her mind, Kate reassembled the brick wall around her private intentions. She would find a way to send a scrap of message to Nan. She would explain. Meanwhile, Kate said to Caterina, "You can tell her I traded my own freedom for hers. She cast me aside, left me to live in basements since I was small. Use that. It will convince her."

"Why should I believe you'd make such a bargain?"

"It's just math. I'm giving up one person to free several. But I want to see the other prisoners file out. I want a window with a view of the forest, where I can see them reach the cover of trees. That's what I'll hold on to. At least until my memory is obliterated. I'll know I did some good for a few people." She pressed her case one notch further. "For Jack."

Wordlessly, Caterina rose, then glided down the length of the table. Kate watched her, waiting and uncertain. Her great-aunt, the witch, slapped her with such force her neck snapped back. Kate gasped.

"I agree to those terms," Caterina announced. "But don't ever presume to make demands of me again."

She reached up to retrieve a polished bell from the shelf to their right. She shook it elegantly, like a hostess bidding her guests to supper. The servant arrived through the far entrance almost immediately. He was built like the ax wielder Kate and Jack had confronted ages ago. Days ago. The servant bowed. He didn't even bother to look directly at the latest addition to his mistress's collection.

"Prepare the prisoners for release," Caterina ordered.

That woke him. He stared up, slack-jawed. "All of them, milady?"

"All of them except my sister." The servant nodded brusquely, but snuck a peek at Kate. He stared in wonder. It shamed Kate to feel a surge of pride. She enjoyed being regarded as a rescuer.

Caterina continued her orders, though, and any vanity Kate had felt evaporated. "You'll need to ready the cell on the third floor, adjacent to my chamber. I wish to be close enough to hear the weeping."

CHAPTER 17

Caterina herself led Kate up the two flights of marble stairs to her readied room. Kate's soft-soled boots didn't make a sound on the smooth floor, but the witch's heels clicked all the way up. At the first landing, Kate considered spinning around, hurtling herself and her captor down the steep stairs. That wouldn't be heroic, though. Caterina had agreed to free the others. Her desperate move would serve only herself.

At first glance, Kate's room did not look like jail. She recognized the stonework from the tapestries. Instead of the iron bench she'd seen in one image, a modest cot stood in the corner. No cushions or carpets anywhere, but Kate had stayed in grimmer quarters.

A window faced east, so she'd have a view of sunrises over the forest. That could taunt her, though, if she allowed herself to recall riding with Jack, with the sun hoisting itself up behind them. Built into the wall, beside the window, iron shackles curled up like a sleeping animal.

"You'll be able to monitor the prisoners' exodus from here."

"They won't see me," Kate stated.

"We didn't set those terms. You'll have to settle for acting as an anonymous benefactor. They'll never know you traded yourself for their liberty." The witch grinned. "You see? You still don't matter."

"Jack will know," vowed Kate.

"Right. As he escorts the gorgeous princess, I'm sure your sacrifice will weigh heavily on his mind."

Kate would not waver. "He'll know."

Caterina just nodded to the chains. "It's time, dear. I might recommend shaking your arms loosely above your shoulders. You won't experience the unrestricted sensation again."

Kate took a step back, feeling the trepidation rising in her chest. "Not until I see them reach the tree line."

The witch rolled her eyes and strode over. Kate winced, expecting to be struck again. But Caterina stepped past her, stood at the top of the staircase, and stamped her foot. "Carry on, please!" she called down, and Kate heard the distant tinkling of keys, of turning locks, in response. "Enjoy your moment, Katherine."

And Kate did. She leaned forward and held on to the window frame with both hands. When she saw the line of stooped shoulders file across the glen, she gripped the wood even tighter. She would not give Caterina the satisfaction of gasping. The figures moved slowly, tentatively—as if they'd lost the ability to confront so much open space. Kate counted four. She recognized the shorn head of a girl from one of the tapestries. She spied auburn curls and the raven-haired beauty who had seemed so frightened by apples. Princess Ella limped behind those three, coaxing the others to move more quickly, even as she kept glancing behind her.

Where could he be? As if he had somehow read her mind, Jack stumbled into her line of vision. She saw his skin was gouged with angry wounds. Caterina's brawny guard drove him forward. Jack kept stopping, fighting his way back. Each time he gained any sort of length, the guard shoved him.

Some of the tears that rolled down Kate's cheeks were tears of happiness. Some were tears of grief. She knew he wouldn't leave her easily. In the field below, Jack sank to his knees. He grabbed fistfuls of his own hair and she could see the wide O of his screaming mouth.

Clear as church bells, Kate heard his keening. He repeated her name over and over. *Katie. Katie.* She shut her eyes and directed all her energy, all the love in her heart toward him.

I know. She hoped those two tiny words would slip through the glass, coast out the window, and float down to him. And they might have. She watched as he caved suddenly, as he hung his head. She saw Ella and the bald prisoner help him up. Frail as the two girls looked, they propped Jack up between them and led him away. The three heads bent together and Kate imagined they might be comforting one another as they made their slow way to the tall oaks.

She did not wait for the witch's order. Kate turned away from the glass and bent to the irons on the floor. Just as she did, she heard the approach of hooves.

They thundered closer and closer. Kate's first thought wasn't even of Jack. She supposed Lucius was coming for her. When she spotted a figure bent forward on a gray horse, tearing across the glen, her mouth dropped open and the shackles fell with a clank.

"What is the meaning of this? If you think for one moment a buzzing little insect like yourself has any prospect of hoodwinking me, of conning me from our acknowledged terms, then you have a whole other reality ready to rain down on you, I swear,"

Caterina raged, even as they both heard the heavy door of the castle crack like a dry piece of kindling.

"You will pay with years of anguish," the witch promised as she stormed from the room and down the stairs. Kate scampered along after her—a little mouse given a brief reprieve from the claws of the cat. She could do little but squeak in shock, looking down into the great hall. There sat Owen Sterling on his dappled steed, brandishing a sword against the chest of Caterina's guard.

"Katherine, come down to me. As quickly as possible." As Sterling spoke, the guard backed away from the blade's point, all the way to the door. He picked through the splinters and sprinted away.

Kate moved gingerly, down one step and then another. Warily, she watched the witch, who heaved and panted with rage.

Sterling kept talking. "Just look at me, Kate. Keep your eyes on me."

But then Caterina spoke and said something strange.

"Joseph Hood. After all these years. You've come for your own."

Hearing the name, Kate swung to face Caterina, who pounced. Grabbing her wrist, Caterina dragged her captive across the last few steps and then down a dank and dark hall.

The corridor was narrow. Sterling had to dismount to give chase. But he did so without hesitation. In the shadows, Kate saw the sword whip past her, an arc of flashing light. Caterina parried, thrusting Kate before her like a shield.

"Is she that disposable to you, Hood? Your long-lost daughter?"

Kate gasped and the witch laughed gleefully.

The constable's eyes reached Kate's, pleading. "She was never lost. She grew up under my watchful eye," he insisted. "I was always near. Checking each roof over your head. Moving you when I had to, from an uncaring landlord or a cruel boss." All the while, Sterling kept up his pursuit, snapping his sword skillfully toward the witch's mocking face. The three of them backed into the cramped darkness—Kate caught between Caterina and the constable, ducking from the blade that kept whistling past her face.

"Ask your father why you had to slave as a servant in the homes of others. Ask him who gave him his new name."

"I am not ashamed," the constable spoke as he advanced. "Kate, I did all I could to save your mother. That meant theft. I stole money to pay a ransom and it would have been worthwhile. But I did make one mistake. I brokered a deal with a witch, who refused to honor her end of the deal."

"Poor Owen Sterling. In debt for the rest of his life. Consider yourself lucky I enchanted an entire village. Otherwise, how would you ever show your unrecognized face? Who would allow you back near their homes, their bank? I always honor my terms." As Caterina insisted on this fact, she choked Kate with one set of fingers, as if for emphasis.

"You paid a ransom and I freed your wife," the witch said. Kate felt each word across her throat. "I'm not to blame because she chose to run." Desperate to breathe, Kate's hand reached behind her, grasping at the bars of the cell at their back.

"My girl would not have chosen to go." Kate heard a voice very much like Caterina's. It whispered. And then she heard another hiss, like a balloon punctured. The witch abruptly loosened her grip on Kate. Both of Caterina's hands, the well and the lame, flew up to her own throat.

Her neck looked as though it was being pierced by a filament of light. Nan had stabbed her sister through the bars of her cell, with the heavy-gauge embroidery needle she'd been forced to use until her fingers bled and her terror had been illustrated. Kate shuddered at the site of the needle quivering. She looked toward the constable, who kept his sword raised, ready to strike and finish the work.

Nan spoke calmly. "Caterina, hand Joseph the keys. You know that I can heal that wound. I swear to you I will. But you must open my cell and the next. Those are the terms of the deal."

They all watched the witch struggle not to scream or swallow. Caterina closed her eyes and seethed. Carefully, steadily, she slipped her hand into her pocket and pulled out the loop of keys. The constable moved quickly, working Nan's lock and then the next. As her cell clicked open, Nan rushed past. She reached for Kate's arm and squeezed. "We have so much to discuss, I know. But right this minute, I need your assistance." Nan looked back at her twin. "After them. I will attend to you after them."

The bodies of the two children lay motionless in the adjacent cell. Nan knelt between them and took a hand of each. She motioned for Kate to do the same.

Kate sucked in her breath sharply; their skin was still hot to the touch. "Don't scare them," Nan instructed. "They must understand it's safe now. Just tell them we'll bring them home to their mother, who misses them. Tell them we'll lead them through the woods and they'll get to ride a horse." Kate opened her mouth to speak. "No," Nan corrected. "Not that way. You must speak to them across a great distance."

Kate stared down at the small, still faces. The girl's blond hair was cut like a boy's, but slightly longer in the back. Kate imagined she wore it short to be more like her brother, whose curls fell in waves over his forehead, around his ears. *Come back,* Kate called from a place deep and buried. *Come home.* She distilled all the power of every cell in her body into those words.

The boy's eyes flickered open first. He dropped Nan's hand and reached immediately for his sister. He'd just grabbed hold of her when she blinked herself awake, too. "Okay, then," Nan said soothingly. "You're just fine. We're all going to go home soon." She nodded to Kate, who took over.

"Your mother will be so relieved to see you. She'll hold you close and hug you tight. The village will want to throw a great big party." Kate looked up at the constable, at her father. "The people will line the streets to welcome you home."

Her father smiled softly down upon her as she rocked the doll-like children. He turned to help hold Caterina down as Nan set out to mend her neck. "Keep still," he ordered.

"Take care," Nan added. "Cat—look at me, please. Cat—I need to push the needle all the way through." Caterina shook her head vigorously, and as she did, tears of pain sprang to her eyes. "I need to, Cat." Out of the corner of her eye, Kate observed her grandmother.

Nan pressed and pulled, finally drawing the needle through the small, round wound. She tied each side with one black stitch so that it looked like a tiny *X* marking a spot on the map of Caterina's neck. She motioned for the constable, who rinsed the laceration with a splash of water from the canteen at his hip. Aside from the low murmuring of the children, the cold dungeon remained quiet.

Kate waited for the witch to rise and rage. "She's passed out from the pain," her father explained. But Kate sneered at the idea of the witch, who had orchestrated the suffering of so many, overcome by what was essentially a pinprick. She stood then, unafraid. Under the careful supervision of her family, Kate crouched over the witch's heavy form. She dragged Caterina back into the cell, stopping only when she reached the manacles bolted to the wall.

"Kate—" her grandmother cautioned.

"Tell me it's not the right thing. Say we all won't be safer this way."

She waited. Nan stayed silent. Caterina came to consciousness just as Kate closed the iron cuff around her one good wrist. "No. No," Caterina croaked. With her other hand, she clawed at Kate. "No, you don't know. *You don't know.*"

Kate stood straight. "I do know. Eventually, the evil you welcomed as part of your self will take over more and more of your own body. You'll be confined, alone in this cell, until one day, it will finally overtake you completely."

"We'll be long gone," Kate declared as she gathered up the two children. "I'm not like you—I don't wish to hear the weeping." With that, Kate turned away and led her charges out into the fresh air of freedom.

EPILOGUE

“That clearing ahead—it looks as good a place as any.” Kate directed the others to a sun-drenched meadow, encircled by tall trees. She, Princess Ella, and Jack urged their horses forward as the other girls raced ahead on foot with their baskets. Behind them, the twin boy and girl pulled a wagon packed with folded blankets. “Thank you kindly!” Kate sang out to them before spreading the blankets on the grass.

Ella set to work arranging the platters of food while Jack tied up the horses. “I promised Lucius an apple,” she said, motioning the younger ones over to help.

The raven-haired girl called out, “Give him mine!”

“Have you named your horse yet, Jack?” Ella asked as she and the twins headed over with treats.

“Your father commanded me to. I wondered who suggested that?”

Kate busied herself with the picnic.

“What is his name?” Hansel asked, offering the brown horse a carrot.

“Kit. My horse’s name is Kit.”

Hansel’s sister looked troubled. “That sounds very much like Kate.”

“Well,” Jack said, his eyes sparkling, “I hadn’t noticed that.” He knelt down to whisper in the girl’s ear. “Can you keep a secret?” She nodded solemnly. “Kit is actually a nickname, based on his initials. And his initials stand for Katherine In Training.”

“But Katherine is a girl’s name!” Gretel shouted in protest before she remembered her vow to secrecy and clamped her hand over her mouth.

“I know, I know. You are absolutely correct. That’s very smart of you. But this is a very special horse. I find him very particular, somewhat frustrating, but altogether necessary to my existence. So he seems like more of a Katherine to me. Do you understand?” Jack asked the little girl, but smiled toward Kate.

“If I didn’t know better, Jack Haricot, I’d say you were bewitched,” the raven-haired girl teased. Initially, the group responded with awkward silence. No one knew quite what to say. But Kate started giggling, then Ella. Jack and the other girls joined in. Even the girl with the short hair, who rarely smiled, chuckled. And the twins, who didn't catch the joke, understood the delight of laughing together.

Kate contemplated her strange, new extended family. Most of them lived with Ella and the king now. Kate lived with her own father and Nan in a house the grateful townsfolk had gifted them. And Jack still lived on his own, revealing the exact location of his dwelling to a select few. Kate gazed at all of them and smiled so wide it almost hurt. She savored their voices, ringing out across the forest in the bright sun.

She heard the weeping only once in a while, persistent sobs echoing from the deepest corner of her mind. She checked sometimes, like poking a scab to find out if the wound had healed. In those times, she heard howls that took hours to shut off.

But not now. More and more, Kate knew how to silence the voice in her head.

She worked hard to surround herself with joyful noise instead.

ACKNOWLEDGMENTS

My son and daughter and I are a team of three, with a formidable support system. I am so grateful for the amazing family and friends who have surrounded us with love, especially over the past few years.

Thank you to David Levithan and the entire Scholastic team for the opportunity to write a fairy tale exactly when I needed one.

ABOUT THE AUTHOR

Elizabeth Paulson lives on the edge of the woods somewhere in America.